I0670452

Nobody's Hero

The Superhero Publicist Book One

Janeen Ippolito

Just Imagine Press

Editing: Sarah McConahy
Typesetting: Sarah Delena White
Cover Art: Kristen Hildebrand
Cover Typography: Enchanted Ink Studio

To my husband Stephen,

my favorite fellow superhero nerd.

CHAPTER ONE

The man staring down at Cassandra was going to be the death of her. Or at least, she could tell he wanted to be. It was clear from the flames in his eyes and the scowl stretching his mouth. Good thing he was on the other side of her desk, his hulking frame overwhelming the gray vinyl-cushioned chair and dominating a corner of her tiny office.

And there she was, barely five foot two and without all the muscles. She would have liked a bulletproof, fireproof see-through barrier between her and the supervillain. Unfortunately, junior marketing representatives didn't get those. A fact that was reinforced by the knives still vibrating in the wall behind Cassie.

Those were from his girlfriend. His partner in crime. Her tight leather ensemble was festooned with flames running down her arms and across the top of her bustier. At least she was wearing a top, unlike her boyfriend next to her. He was clad only in tight leather pants and motorcycle boots.

Cassie bit back her comments. Supervillains were allowed to wear whatever they liked at Power-Up Publicity. Picking the right battles was ground-floor knowledge, and her office was in the basement.

"Have I made myself clear, trash?" Flaze cracked his meaty knuckles. "My girl gets to use whatever alias she wants."

"It's my favorite movie!" the genner who wanted to be known as Flashdance whined, picking at her fingernails. "She's so elegant and"—she sniffled— "my guy met me the same way."

Cassie paused. "You were a cabaret singer at a bar he owned?"

"No." The blonde drew out the word with another sniffle. "He was in charge of my first smash-and-grab and, well, after I saw him light up that dumpster of explosives, the rest was history." She sighed, hand over her heart, her expression dreamy.

Flaze turned to her, his countenance suddenly soft. "Aw, babe, you'll always be my little firefly."

"And you're my firecracker." She ran her fingers through his spiky, white-bleached hair with black roots.

Cassie's stomach churned.

No. No vomiting. It would mess up her wastebasket and maybe get more knives thrown at her. Instead, she dabbed at the cut on her face, managed to put on a bandage without looking, took a sip of her Mountain Dew, and searched her mind for the best words. They could be her last. With the clients her supervisors sent her way, she could be dead any day now.

God, help me find something to say.

She should try the legal route. "The fact remains that the movie title is copyrighted and, understandably, they wouldn't want it associated with your ... particular activities."

"'Understandably?'" Flaze turned back to her, his massive biceps flexing. "What're you saying?"

Flames rose high on his arms, increasing the room temperature. He wanted a fight. And she was almost out of burn cream and flame-retardant spray.

She tugged at the tip of her high ponytail. Maybe a calm, firm response would work.

"You have excellent hearing, Flaze." She set her jaw. "You hired me to work for you and your best interests. Part of my job is helping you avoid any unwanted publicity issues."

"But my beefcake sparkplug gets to have *his* name!" Flashdance crossed her arms and pouted.

That's because no one else wants it. Cassie swallowed down the words. "His name is available on the trademark registry and isn't used by any business with enough clout to attempt a legal battle."

"What about a real battle?" Flaze punched one hand into another.

"That isn't my department, sir." She tapped one purple manicured finger on the tablet computer on the desk between her and her clients. "Please select a new name from the list of available possibilities. Some of them, I think, would work out well."

He eyed the tablet skeptically. "What would you know about rad names? You might have purple hair, but you're still a pencil pusher."

"Another part of my job, Mr. Flaze." Really, she would rather call him anything else, but he had opted not to list his real name on his forms, and his girlfriend had done likewise. Probably the pair could barely cover their fees. Might even have been given a generous discount by Power-Up Publicity. Anything for corporate to get more clients who might one day make it big and have more money.

Flashdance picked up the tablet with one hand, chewing her lip. "Hmmm. Oh look, baby, this one might work—ow!"

Her free hand slapped over her ear, and flames spurted from her fingertips, melting the edges of the tablet.

Cassie hurriedly grabbed the device back. "A problem?"

It was probably an inconspicuous earbud communicator. The techies were making them smaller and smaller. She'd heard that some were trying to create nanotech implants.

"Yeah, got some bad things to do." Flaze gave a sneer that was more annoyed walrus than deadly supervillain. His flames and weapons were all too real, though, so she kept her mouth shut. "Get back to this later, ord trash."

Ord. Standard slang for ordinaries—those without any superpowers. But coming out of Flaze's mouth, it was a profanity.

"It's Ms. Robinson." Cassie stood to her full height and tugged down her black blazer. "Remember that, Mr. Flaze, or you will find another publicist."

"Yeah, yeah. Sure. We both know the company has us on your docket for life. Until the end of yours." He took his girlfriend's hand and pulled her to her feet, yanking her close. "Come on, my little firefly. It's time to burn."

Flashdance giggled, staring up at him adoringly. "Oh, I love when you say that."

They left her office, their boots clomping on the floor.

Once the sound was out of earshot, Cassie strode to her

office door and clicked all the deadbolts and locks into place. Representatives with higher status had the latest in force field technology from proprietary in-house laboratories. She had to settle for endless locks that could be opened remotely if her supervisors deemed it necessary, a metal door heavy enough to be in a maximum-security prison, and an array of security cameras that would either alert security to help her or document her last moments.

Thanks to the papers I signed, my parents can't even sue them. Not that they would anyway. Her parents wanted nothing to do with her marketing work. They didn't even know she was hooked into Power-Up Publicity's terrible deal.

How was it that Congress had finally created a department for dealing with genners, but there weren't any laws against her situation?

Mom and Dad would be even more fed up about me wanting government regulations. She trudged back to her desk and her soda, her fingers shaking. *But they aren't here. I am.*

After another restorative chug that steadied the shaking, she leaned back in her chair. Time to take some notes and get herself together. Maybe pray that the rest of the villains on her schedule didn't throw knives. At least none of them had done major damage, although some had missed killing her by millimeters. That kind of unbelievable luck had to be a sign that there was still a plan for her beyond this ambush of a job.

She glanced up at the blades still jammed in the wall. Would Flashdance and Flaze want them back? They generally threw a lot of knives, and she always kept them. Auctioning them off online could help supplement her income.

"No, Cassie. Bad idea." The villain duo could find her on eBay and take her out. Or Power-Up Publicity could do something terrible to her. She groaned. "How is this job a good idea?"

It wasn't. None of this had been in the plans. She'd ditched law school for marketing and communications. She wanted to work with genners, a common term for those with genetics that predisposed them to superpowers—some of them with major help from test-tube formulas. A genner had saved her life, after all, and the official viral video Emergence had happened during her first semester at Northwestern. However, top marks in an irrelevant pre-law major and a basic online degree weren't enough to impress any businesses until Power-Up Publicity. But somehow, instead of getting hero work, they'd switched up her contract so she had to work with villains. If she succeeded in her first year, they'd start letting her work with the good guys.

Cassie had realized after her first day that success meant simply surviving. Some of her coworkers didn't. Hadn't survived. According to the contract, all junior representatives with villain clients waived holding Power-Up Publicity liable.

What kind of place is this? She didn't speak it aloud. Rumor was the cameras had an audio recording component. All of the marketing firm's work was way too Big Brother for her tastes. They even provided her with a utilitarian apartment, which she had been encouraged to use. When she hadn't moved into it, her old place had developed bed bugs, electrical wiring issues, and plumbing backups within days, leaving her no choice but the company option. Except for Katrina. But there was no way she'd make it safely to Katrina's haven before someone at Power-Up Publicity found her.

Found her? Would they really hunt her down?

It had to be a conspiracy.

Great. Now I sound like Mom and Dad. She groaned again. This was her life right now.

"Buck up and deal with it," she muttered, reaching for the tablet. "At least they didn't fry this." Otherwise, she would've had to deal with Requisitions, and they already blamed her for the cell-phone-meets-ceiling-fan incident. An incident that was not her fault. Not that any logic had appeased them.

She flipped through the tablet for her next client. They weren't due for two hours. Goody. Cassie yawned, suddenly exhausted. Her work kept her life interesting—and also drained her a lot. There was time to collect the knives and drink another Mountain Dew. She should probably turn on the air conditioning to deal with the residual heat, although it felt nice to her. She was perpetually cold. But it was better to wear extra layers than to upset a supervillain.

Cassie flipped open a compact and did a quick makeup check. She adjusted some of the olive-toned foundation powder around the dot-shaped Band-Aid, then snapped the compact closed. Maybe once she survived, then she could work with heroes. Instead of coming up with promotional ideas that would somehow amplify her clients' villainous plans while not actually endorsing them, she could come up with marketing strategies for the good guys.

Meanwhile, she was helping villains. Cassie had already been tainted. Really, was there even a point in hoping?

She opened her inbox. The usual subject lines about new clients, adjustments to corporate policy, and one from Human Resources, reminding her that she only had two months left in her supervillain work.

"Continue with the excellent work, Ms. Robinson. You have the potential for great things, and great things are coming your way," Cassie read aloud. Then she blinked. "And a sideways smiley face?"

She shook her head. The ending sounded like a fortune cookie. Someone in HR had a weird sense of humor. Or were they trying to flirt with her? No, it looked like a standard form email.

This company was getting weirder and more messed-up by the day.

Cassie played with the tiny pendant of a spine around her neck. A spine. Sure, her actual spine was okay now, except for some lingering aches and stiffness. The spine support pillow on her chair helped with that and, well, she'd always lived with some random body aches.

As far as a moral spine ... wouldn't it be nice to have one of those again instead of just trying to survive?

"Enough moping." Cassie picked up her wireless headphones and turned on an upbeat playlist. "If you can't beat 'em, collect the weapons they tried to kill you with, then focus on the next person."

Chapter Two

"Stop! In the name of the law!"

"What law?" Mick muttered under his breath as he ducked down against the wall. "There's no law against stealing black market goods."

Or at least, there shouldn't be. It was absolute idiocy to enforce any kind of law that protected fat cats and crime lords from someone stealing and freeing their wrongfully acquired trade secrets. Or art. Or people, because human trafficking of that kind happened sometimes between scumbags.

Not that stealing was on the agenda today. All he'd wanted to do was get to Power-Up Publicity.

That was ironic in itself.

He peered around the corner. Great, there was a full lineup of supposed good guys in makeshift outfits that revealed which ones had wealthy sponsors or an inheritance and which ones were DIY with scraps of leather and spandex. One was in jeans, a zip-up hoodie, and a Pokémon shirt. *Way to represent.*

Mick would try to avoid the gamer dude. Really, he wasn't supposed to be hurting anyone beyond self-defense or the protection of others. But the random heroes of St. Louis were making that hard, although at least they hadn't caused property damage yet. If they did, it would be caught on camera—there were already three bystanders with phones out, while others just moved to opposite sidewalks. Ords realized quickly that it was best to stay out of the way unless they had an online video channel or were trying to get footage for a lawsuit.

"Come out, Swipe," intoned a barrel-chested man with a cape and a flashy gold star emblazoned on his red unitard. "You're in a dead end."

The woman next to him in a black bodysuit and mask scoffed. "A dead-end life too. More counts of larceny than I've ever seen. On top of that, manslaughter and murder—"

"And tax evasion!" That came from the one with the snail-like eye stalks, which swiveled back and forth, and the shell on his back. The rest of him looked humanoid, so maybe the head was an experiment gone wrong? Or powers by damage. "You may think you are too fast for justice, but justice will always find you!"

Great pep talk. Absolutely feel like turning myself in. Not that they'd care why he stole things, or that sometimes the situations were a setup, or that he'd never killed an innocent person, only other criminals and only as an absolute last resort.

The tax evasion ... they had him on that one. He should probably feel more convicted about it than he did.

Icy air blasted around the corner, tossing Mick's hair around his head. Thanks to one of the superheroes, Frostblight. He sighed. Enough of this. He needed to get out of here. It gnawed at him that he'd been ambushed in the first place—he'd been so careful.

Maybe someone in the lineup of do-gooders had super-senses. Heightened smell was always tricky to deal with. And apparently Snailman had it out for him. Jealousy, perhaps?

God, I know I'm not in the right here, but I'm trying to do something right. Get me to the next step. Running couldn't last forever, but at least it would get him a little farther.

Sucking in a breath, he focused on where he needed to go. Doing so was important when he had to shift from zero to high octane. Down two streets, off to the left, around a billboard advertising protective gear for genner fights. And right into Power-Up Publicity, which worked with both heroes and villains and was neutral territory, at least so far. As soon as Mick was inside, he had temporary asylum, and he could get on with his real goal: figuring out why Donny wanted him there in the first place.

Ice shards blasted around the corner, aiming vaguely in his direction. A telekinetic on the team as well? Not a good one. That was the problem with all the random superhero groups, tag-team-ups, and solo acts—no dedication to craft. The supervillain gangs were generally more organized. For bad reasons, but still.

One. Two.

Five.

Mick started off at his highest speed, zipping around the heroes and resisting the urge to literally run circles around them. His cargo pants still had a rip from the last time he'd done that and gotten scorched by a fire genner. The injury had healed fine, but it wasn't worth repeating.

Down Fifth Street and Sixth Street. Left at the five-story glass-and-burgundy stone building with Power-Up Publicity emblazed near the top in silver lettering. Through the glass double doors, pulling them closed behind him.

The world came into focus around Mick. His heart thudded in his chest. Sprint speed was exhilarating, but also took it out of him. How many days of life had he lost in that sprint? Three days? Five?

It wasn't worth thinking about. He liked his powers, no matter the cost of using them—and no one really knew when their time would come anyway.

A corporate jungle surrounded him. Literally, in the case of the hideous abstract art sculptures filling the cavernous lobby. Whoever had designed them should have their fingers shot off as a service to humanity, or at least humanity's eyeballs.

I've shot off fingers. The hard truth of that stopped his line of thought cold. Mick had done what he had to do to survive, and the other super had survived as well. It had been gang-on-gang violence.

That didn't make it any better.

Mick clenched his fists inside his brown leather jacket. There was no taking back the past. He could only live better for now and be thankful that there was grace even for people like him. Someone who should've known better and made a damn fool of himself anyway.

Even so, his muscles twitched with the urge to run and not stop. This monstrous building was the last place he wanted to be. If it was empty of people, he'd happily see it destroyed.

He paced over to one of the silver mirrors hanging on a smooth gray wall. The mirror was blurred and distorted in decorative swirls. It warped his tanned face and black hair, but probably hid a security device. The obvious places were the best.

Mick turned and paced back toward the small cluster of uncomfortable chairs.

First step was finding out what was going on with Donny. Usually his brother's tip-offs had more focus to them. A plan to sabotage. Some documents to take and drop off anonymously to organizations that could help. People to rescue.

Not this one. Mick pulled out his encrypted phone and opened the text again. *Power-Up Publicity. Supervillain publicist division.* Then the address for this particular location.

There hadn't been any texts since, and no answer to his question for more info. The latter was troubling. Donny usually replied, even if it was just snark.

He squared his shoulders. Deal with the tip-off first. Then he'd see what was up with his brother.

Mick walked up to the reception area. He hadn't made an appointment, but it was probably best to pretend that he was here on official business before launching into full speedster powers and racing through the building looking for answers. That was the extent of his plans. His speed should be able to get him out of this place, no problem.

A stocky bald man with brown skin stood behind the polished black marble counter with metallic bronze earbuds in both ears and fingers working at three keyboards with three different screens.

A genner with a tech power, or a highly skilled ord?

Before Mick could speak, the guy beat him to it.

"Go to the first hallway on the right, down the ramp, last door on the left in the supervillain publicist hallway. Ms. Robinson." His voice was warm and raspy. He was maybe late fifties, wearing a nondescript black suit and white shirt. With easy movements, he placed a white, plastic-coated badge on the counter. "Wear this at all times when in the building."

"How did you know?" The receptionist hadn't even looked up from the screens.

"I'm monitoring the cameras, Swipe." There was gentle remonstrance in his tone. "We don't leave matters to chance here. Good day."

Mick frowned. This was weird. Was the company tracking him? They shouldn't be. Donny took care of that.

At last, the receptionist looked up. His eyes were the same metallic bronze of his earbuds. "Ms. Robinson. Last door on the left." He paused, his right eye twitching slightly. "With all speed, Swipe."

"Yeah, okay." Mick grabbed the badge, turning it over in his hand and examining every part quicker than breath. Whatever tech was in this, it couldn't be detected by the naked eye.

Run. The receptionist was giving him instant appointments. It had to be a setup.

No. With a tiny exhale, he forced his tense muscles to calm. He was here to get answers, and the receptionist was just making that easier. Of course they would know he was Swipe. But they didn't know how fast he actually was. He always used the minimum speed needed for any job. It was best to keep enemies in the dark about your true power level.

He still had the advantage here. Donny wanted him to check out supervillain publicity anyway.

Mick strode across the lobby and down the hallway, forcing himself to keep a normal pace. It would be stupid to burn out his energy getting to the doorway. Better play out this scenario first. Maybe he'd learn something from how they treated supervillains here that would help with ... he had no idea.

Or things could tank. Badly. Still, he had to spare a little for hope, even some divine intervention. Or else what was he even doing here?

Mick stopped in front of a gray metal door identical to the other ones on this floor. No windows. No art or even wallpaper. Just plain white walls and doors that looked like they came off a bank vault.

Were they trying to trap the supervillains in or the publicists?

The space between his shoulder blades itched.

Didn't matter. Mick set his jaw.

He was going in.

Chapter Three

Before he could rethink, he grabbed the door handle and yanked it open. On the other side was a petite woman in a black business suit balanced on a computer chair behind a large white desk in a beige-colored room. Besides the usual office stuff on the desk, there was a placard with her name on it—Ms. Robinson, Junior Representative—and a small plastic sunflower bobbing sideways in a tiny pot. The time read 10 a.m, and the place smelled faintly like...smoke?

She jerked away from the monitor and blinked. "Excuse me, but ... who are you?"

"Your ten o'clock, I guess."

"I don't have a ten o'clock. How did you get in the door?" She picked up a dented tablet computer and swiped at the screen. Her nose wrinkled, then she sighed. "Ah, I ... see. Mr. Brown. It seems you were a last-minute addition—which explains the receptionist disabling the locks." Under her breath, the junior representative muttered, "Thanks, Angus."

There was something familiar in how she smacked her lips in annoyance, then picked at the edges of her purple manicured nails. Huh. Why would that be familiar? Painted nails were a waste of time, but it wasn't like he really cared.

Still, somehow he was sure she needed to be teased.

Mick nodded at the sunflower. "Couldn't afford a real one, Ms. Robinson?"

"A real one would die in here," was her flat answer. The woman stared up at him from beneath purple bangs. "It isn't the season for them, anyway. It's spring."

"Are you some kind of botanist?" Mick stepped into the room, making sure to keep one hand on the door so it stayed open. A little curiosity didn't mean he could let his guard down. "Have a plant power?"

Dumb response. He was supposed to just get in and out with a quick investigation, not waste time with banter. But something in her brown eyes provoked him. How was she still alive if she talked that way to other supervillains?

Maybe she was a genner after all. Not all genners had abilities useful for big-time work.

"I have no powers. Except for stating the obvious, but you started it, so I think you have me beat." She sighed again, turned to her computer, and typed away. Her eyes scanned the screen. "*Swipe*, is it? You're welcome to come all the way inside."

He grabbed one of the two chairs in front of her desk, used one to prop open the door, then settled into the other one, shoving his shoes up on the edge of her desk, just to see what would happen.

"Ready to go."

"Of course you are." That dry gaze stared at his shoes. But no words came out, at least none about his intrusion. Instead, she gave

17

him a syrupy smile. "If you'll just give me one minute? I need to look over your materials, since you were added very recently."

Well, that made sense. Hopefully it wouldn't take too long. He had places to be. Specifically, all over the supervillain publicist area, as fast as his powers could take him. Absently, he took in the neat stacks and folders on her desk. One of them was anchored by a small stone paperweight of a dragon.

"Do you like dragons?"

"Hm? They're ... whatever." She shrugged, picking up a tablet computer. "That paperweight was a cheap thrift store find."

She was lying. Something in the way she touched her lips, painted with dark lipstick. The way her eyebrow raised, just a little. She loved dragons. The thrift store thing might've been true, but her dismissal of dragons wasn't.

How do I know that? Mick shrugged and leaned back in the seat. It didn't matter to him. He wasn't here to figure out a junior representative.

Still, he had nowhere else to look, so he studied Ms. Robinson, arms folded across his chest. The rest of her long hair was the same purple as her fingernails. Olive skin with warm yellow undertones, a heart-shaped face that came to a sharp chin, and those thin, mirkish lips, still twitching as she flipped through the documents.

An image flashed in his mind, turning into a memory. *That face, only covered in acne. Choppy black hair flopped around her face instead of pulled back, and her eyes squinting in concentration as she smeared dark lipstick on her lips.*

He made a face at her, and she paused to stick her tongue out at him.

"Knock it off, Mikey." The woman—girl who already looked like a woman—rolled her eyes. "You'll make me get it on my braces."

"Too late." He grinned.

She shoved him playfully. "You jerk!"

"I don't know why you bother. Mr. Dibner will just make you take it off anyway."

"But until then, I'm my own person. And I like it." She pursed her lips. "What? Does it look creepy?"

"Yeah, you're a vampire now."

"Mwahaha ..."

The lipstick hadn't looked creepy. It had suited her features, just like it did now. Made her look older and professional. Although now she *was* older, by thirteen years.

Hell. Cassandra Royas, right in front of him. Or at least, her doppelganger. Those did happen once in a while. Or a shapeshifter who, for some reason, liked this form. No, that didn't make sense.

But why would she go by Robinson? Better to play this on the downlow until he had more information. Just because they'd been inseparable over a decade ago didn't mean anything now.

Although ... had he told Donny about her? Maybe a little. It couldn't have been that much. Not enough for his half-brother to send him here for her. Besides, why not use her name?

"All right, Swipe." She looked up from the tablet computer. "It says here that you're a supervillain with powers of speed, enhanced motion, reflexes, and healing."

"All true." Since he was officially a test-tube genner, that data was out there for anyone to find. But there were other powers he wouldn't admit to just anyone. Including the side effects.

"You've been associated with the Lascivious League, the Starspires, the Fireballs, and the ... Too-ath?"

"Tuath," he corrected, with the pronunciation *twath*. "Irish gang. Leaders had sonic powers."

Ms. Robinson made a note with a stylus on the tablet. "Right. You've been accused of murder—"

Mick sat up, but still managed to keep his shoes on her desk. "It's not murder when the other person tried to kill you first. And one time, some punk was after kids. That doesn't count either."

"Fine. Killing people, then."

"Better." Not that he was proud of killing them. Just one of many things he had to live with, pushed into a corner of his mind and lifted up in prayer on bad nights.

He'd tried his best, off and on. No matter what the official documents said, he wasn't really a villain. He'd never crossed those final lines. Just gone antihero for a while, then tried to help people outside the law, which sometimes meant working with the bad guys and ignoring dumb rules. Considering those rules protected places like Power-Up Publicity, he didn't feel guilty about it.

Ms. Robinson looked up. "We can debate it later." From her tone, it almost sounded like she meant it. She would have, in the past, when she was Cassie Royas. Who knew now? "You're also implicated in a number of thefts and break-ins at various locations."

"You have to see someone to prove that or have DNA evidence."

Those scenes were clean. He'd made sure of it.

"One complaint from a building manager stating that you removed most of the lounge furniture from the top deck and installed an unauthorized lock on the door."

Mick shrugged. "I wanted some time alone. I uninstalled it when I moved out a week later. And repaired one of the Adirondack chairs."

"Gold stars for you." She rolled her eyes and swiped through the tablet. "All right, how can I help you?"

Her eyes drifted to his shoes on her desk once more. Mick smiled slightly and moved his feet back to the floor. Her shoulders slumped a little, but otherwise, she made no reaction. Well, that was different. The old Cass would have been making sarcastic remarks as soon as he messed with her desk.

People changed over time. She thought he was a supervillain because he was, technically. Although, not really. Still, as an ord, her restraint was probably a good thing.

Did she even recognize him? Mick thought back to his twelve-year-old self. Pudgy. Buzzed hair. About a foot shorter than his height of six feet now. Glasses, which he'd worn before getting the genner procedure.

Yeah, he'd looked a little different.

"Well, Mr. Brown, why are you here? What is so urgent to get a last-minute appointment?"

He sought for an excuse. For some reason, he wanted to talk with Cass a bit more, even if it was one-sided. Donny had sent him the location for this specific supervillain publicist department. Now here was his old friend, looking peeved and discouraged beneath her makeup. He could still read her enough to see that.

"I'm quitting," he said finally.

"Quitting what?"

"Being a supervillain."

Chapter Four

Ms. Robinson froze. "You don't want to be a supervillain anymore?"

"That's what I said."

"... Is this some kind of joke?" She dropped her pencil on her desk, eyes darting around the room and toward the open doorway. "If it is, it isn't funny!"

Mick wrinkled his brows. "Why would it be a joke?"

"You're right. Maybe a test instead. Well, I'm not falling for it." She set the tablet on the desktop. "Mr. Swipe, you're in the wrong place. I'm not allowed to work with superheroes until I survive my twelve-month contract."

He blinked, his mind quickly spinning through her words and the implications. "You say 'survive.' Is your life in danger?"

"No. Yes. Sometimes." She gave him a thin smile. "I do work with *supervillains*."

"But if you're meant to do what I say, why can't you just work with me as well?" That kind of rule-bending would have been fine with the old Cass. He'd been the one who was more of a stickler back at school, if the rules made sense. Cass had always taken those rules as a challenge.

"Certain things are off-limits." She sighed. "There must have been a mix-up. I want to work with heroes, but Power-Up Publicity requires a stint in supervillain work first." Ms. Robinson fiddled with her pen. "No one wants to work with them. With you. High turnover rate."

"Due to death."

"Or permanent disability. Or sometimes psychosis. Although the last one is hard to prove to HR and collect benefits."

Mick scowled. Typical of big corporations, especially when work with genners still wasn't regulated much except that you couldn't help the villains commit crimes. Technically, Power-Up Publicity was simply offering a variety of marketing and branding services, not abetting any criminal activity. The CEO Max Fields was a corporate creephole of the worst degree. "Why would you sign a contract for a job like that?"

Cass's family had been off the grid. Corporate seemed the opposite of her style—or at least, it had been back then. Had she changed that much?

Her expression softened and her voice lowered. "I really want to work with superheroes. Ever since ... well, one saved my life, and then later was blacklisted and forced out of work just because someone didn't like her. How dumb is that?"

"Yeah, dumb." It happened all the time. It was a reason he'd never bothered with a marketing platform or trying to prove himself to anyone. Didn't matter what you said or did. All it took was someone with a better spokesperson or a better lawyer and they could tank you.

Let them call him a villain. He knew his own limits.

"So, you're a ... marketing hero for heroes?"

"I mean, I want to be." Ms. Robinson shrugged. "I don't have powers, but I know how to work with people. Still, I only had an associate degree, and I'd run out of money for school. Then Power-Up Publicity made me an offer." She pressed her lips together. "I don't know why I'm telling you this."

Dang, she really didn't remember him. A part of him wanted to tell her right then. But she was working for a suspicious organization, and it had been thirteen years. Who knew if this was a set-up? It was unlikely. It was more likely this was somehow Donny's doing or just a coincidence, but it didn't hurt to be careful.

He gave her a blank look. "My natural charm and engaging demeanor."

"Sure, that's it."

"Well, sounds like signing the contract was stupid."

"Thank you, Captain Obvious. Maybe that should be your new alias." Ms. Robinson pointed toward the door. "Like I said, I can't work with superheroes. Have a nice day."

Giving up this easy? Either this was an act and she was out to get him ... or they really had something on her.

Mick stood up and brushed off his jeans. Something was off. People changed, but this? It wasn't a change. It was a trap, and it seemed like Cass was caught in it. Corporate was just as bad as gang life, only with more brochures and ugly-ass sculptures. He needed to speed them out of this joint altogether. He could come back later to research his brother's tip if it was something different.

If she was as stubborn as she'd been in school, she wouldn't ask for help.

A glint caught his eye. He paused.

"Is that a spine pendant around your neck?"

"Yes." She was already turning back to the tablet computer.

His heart clenched. She still had the necklace, after all this time. And it didn't look scuffed or tarnished, even though it hadn't been that expensive. His allowance hadn't been much.

No way could he leave without giving her a way out too. Cass needed help.

But how could he get her away from this cage?

"Hey, do you want to take this outside?"

"What? I mean, excuse me?" Ms. Robinson blinked. "I told you, I can't work—"

"Maybe I've changed my mind again. If I were to keep being a supervillain, would you talk with me outside? I need some fresh air."

"We're supposed to meet all clients within this building. For our own protection."

For the security cameras, more than likely.

"I don't care. You're supposed to work with me, and I'm done being inside. I get claustrophobic after a while. It's the speedster thing. Also, I'm hungry. There's a burger truck out there, and a shawarma truck. A few others too." He wasn't ravenous, but with how his powers worked, he could always eat something.

She checked her cell phone. "You only have forty minutes left.

We couldn't go far."

"I walk fast, remember?" Would she just take a hint?

Maybe she wouldn't. If she was smart, she'd be suspicious of all supervillains, even those who claimed they wanted to quit. Especially if they doubled back a few moments later.

"Fine." She rose to her feet and tugged down her blazer. Her head only came up to his shoulder, even with the chunky heels, and the business suit hugged more curves than he'd seen from behind the desk. Then she grabbed a cross-body purse. "Lead the way, Swipe."

"Do you have a weapon in there?"

"If I did, I wouldn't tell you."

"Good." She might have a chance of surviving whatever he had planned.

As soon as he finished planning it.

Chapter Five

This was a bad idea. It had to be. Going along with any supervillain outside was a sure way to die before the end of her contract. Never mind that he claimed he wanted to switch to being a hero—he could back down just as quickly. All of this could just be a mind game for unknown awful reasons. Or he could simply kill her for the fun of it.

Cassie traced a ridged scar on her wrist, one of a number she'd received while working at Power-Up Publicity.

Would Swipe add another one?

No. He wouldn't. He would never.

A gut instinct? Well, her gut could be wrong.

This one is different. There was something in his dark eyes, the way he'd bluntly owned up to his crimes. Swipe wasn't trying too hard. He was barely trying at all, which fit what she'd learned of his character from her quick review. A flight risk through and through.

But he hadn't left her office, at least not alone.

Cassie stayed beside him as they walked down the hallway, taking extra steps because his legs were way longer than hers. As she passed other doorways, her coworkers glanced at her curiously.

One drew his index finger across his throat in a slicing motion.

In trouble? Or dead? Perhaps, although not directly. Job termination could result from going outside with Swipe, but not the permanent kind of termination. She would have noticed that in the contract.

Still, her bosses could easily put her in the way of an accident. Would they?

Could she trust anyone here?

Swipe wants to be a hero. He seemed to actually care that she was in a crappy situation. That was ... kinda heroic. Or he could be a psychopath playing on her vulnerability for his own amusement. That was far more likely.

Wouldn't a psychopath be smoother, though? Swipe wasn't pretending to be a Prince Charming type. It was refreshing, in an odd way.

Hopefully it wouldn't turn deadly.

She rubbed her palms against the sides of her business suit, then stilled her hands as they walked into the lobby. Angus gave her a small wave and smile from reception, where he worked seemingly all the time. Even when Cassie pulled all-nighters, he had still been there at the desk. The only time he took breaks was for the bathroom or once a week for a dinner date with someone he called "his special friend." The standing belief in the office was that he was some kind of realistic android, not that those existed.

"Hi, Angus." She returned his wave and smile. "I'm taking a walk with a potential client."

He raised one black eyebrow a fraction. "Outside?"

"File it under 'special client demands.' I should still have some leeway there."

"Indeed." Angus lifted his head and gave Swipe a firm stare. "Do you know how to behave, young man?"

Cassie braced herself for a snarky remark from Swipe.

"My goal is her care." His words were brusque. She fought the urge to look up and see if he was actually serious or just being sarcastic.

It could be both. With her, it was sometimes both, so perhaps he was the same. Something seemed familiar about their banter, but she would have remembered someone who looked like a quarterback with tanned skin, a square jaw, and black hair swept across his forehead. Especially with the handful of tattoos scattered around.

The receptionist typed at his keyboard. "Then you need to turn in that badge, Swipe."

"Wait, we'll be back—"

"Here." Swipe dropped it on the counter. "All right, let's go."

As they made their way to the double doors at the front of the building, his pace sped up, and so did hers.

"Really hungry for lunch, aren't you?" she asked.

"Always. I eat like a pregnant blue whale."

"How would you know, Cousteau?"

Swipe flashed her a grin as he pushed through the door. "I'm a man of unexpected interests, Ms. Robinson."

"Marine biology, huh? Or maybe you could speed-walk on water. The Jesus connotation could help. If you are trying to become a superhero, that is."

He smirked. "Good to know."

Cassie sighed. *God, please don't let this be a bad idea.*

Outside, they made for Kiener Plaza Park, and she surveyed the various food trucks. Including Casa de Marco, the elusive taco truck with new fusion flavors every week. The truck was only here once a week and never at the same time. But it didn't matter. There was always a line around the corner.

Once they reached the park, a new truck selling burgers was the closest. She wasn't the biggest fan—they tended to be greasy, and the fries didn't have enough salt—but it would make for the easiest getaway. Given that this could be a trap, greasy burgers were the safest bet.

Not that she was much safer inside Power-Up Publicity, but at least she knew who the enemy was.

Cassie gestured to the burger truck. "Here we are—"

"Let's do the taco truck near the park benches." He nodded in that direction, pulling his hood over his hair. Afraid of the law? Well, he *was* a supervillain.

"These burgers are decent."

"You've eyed the taco truck at least twice."

Cassie tilted her head to the side. "Checking me out, huh?"

"Situational awareness is smart. After all, you could be lying to me about being a poor employee trapped at a sleazy firm." He started toward the taco truck. One second he was at the edge of the curb, and quicker than a blink, he was on the other side of the street.

"Are you coming?" he called.

Annoying show-off. But there was something in his calculated expression that said he was testing her. Measuring her.

Well, he could wait, then.

She slowly, deliberately strolled over to the curb, waited for the walking signal even though she would normally have jaywalked. When the light turned green, she took a slow breath of the fresh spring air and leisurely stretched her arms over her head before strolling over to him. By the time she reached him, he was sitting on one of the benches in an isolated part of the park with two large plastic bags filled with several cardboard containers. Two large paper cups rested on the ground next to him.

Cassie sat on the bench catty-corner to his. "That line is fifteen people long. Sure you didn't just help yourself?"

"Of course I did." Swipe wolfed down a taco in a few seconds. Speed eating—not on the list, but to be expected. Speedsters burned through calories, and he would have to eat extra to keep any kind of muscle mass. Typically, a speed genner was a stick. "Around the back of the truck, where they have extras made up, and I paid double what they were charging."

"Oh. Well, that works." Cassie glanced at one of the bags. The mouthwatering scents of barbacoa, melted cheese, and fresh salsa wafted from it. "Since you're being charitable, I'll just help myself—"

"No." His hand caught hers and held fast. Warmth spread through her, along with a jolt of fear. The super's gaze was deadly serious.

What had she been thinking? Supervillains could be weird about their food.

Never show fear. At least, not to this one. On occasion, a bit of groveling was a good idea, but this guy didn't seem the type to respect that.

Instead, she kept her voice light. "Taco monster, huh? New handle?"

"You might need an empty stomach." Swipe leaned in close. She could smell something vaguely like menthol—maybe deodorant? Running fast would make him sweat. Or would it, if his entire metabolism was altered?

It didn't matter.

"Why would I need an empty stomach?"

"In case you didn't notice, I travel very fast. It tends to make ords nauseous."

"Uh huh," she answered, neutral.

She wasn't going anywhere with Swipe.

You can trust him. Nope, that gut instinct had to be wrong. Blame the lack of calories. It had been a while since breakfast.

"I can get you out of here," he whispered. "Away from Power-Up Publicity. New identity, money. Everything you need for a fresh start."

Her mouth dropped open. "What? What are you talking about?"

Swipe's lips twitched. "You act tough, but if you're really in danger, this is your ticket out."

"Is this some kind of weird supervillain fantasy? Rescue the publicist-in-distress?" Cassie frowned up at him. "You can't be serious."

"As I said, I'm not a villain anymore."

"You need to talk with yourself from five minutes ago. Or ten. Whatever." Familiar or not, gut instinct or not, she needed to get off this guy's radar. At the very least, he wasn't stable. The way his dark eyes flitted around suggested he was making this up as he went along.

Because he always did when he was nervous. Tensed up like a cornered animal, ready to strike if necessary.

Where had that come from?

"What the crap, Cass?" he huffed. "Do you always have to give a comeback?"

"Only when I'm facing an out-of-his-mind supervillain—wait, what did you call me?"

No one called her that. It was always Cassie. That was her preference, since Cassandra was just … long.

Only one person called her Cass, and she'd left him behind when she'd moved away from the Lifer school.

"No time to explain. I can't leave you in there." He grabbed her other arm, not restricting her movements, but as if he really was ready to run with her.

Cassie licked her lips, her mind whirling. This couldn't be Mikey. He was too tall and too built and— "How did you get powers?"

"Later, Cass. I promise." He leaned in a little more. "Trust me."

Her heart quickened. *I can't believe I'm considering this.* He could be a shapeshifter masquerading as her old friend. Or some kind of complicated illusion. Or all of this could just be a messed-up dream in her head.

But what if it was real? What if this was the out she'd been hoping for? Praying for?

She took a breath. Exhaled.

"All right, how—"

"Unhand her, you fiend!"

Cassie turned toward the resonant, almost echoey voice.

Before her stood a giant ... what was that?

A snailman.

CHAPTER SIX

A wave of clear slime blasted toward Mick.

Not just at him. At Cass. Stupid hero couldn't even aim right.

Mick shoved her back, away from the stream, then sped backward himself. A stray glop of slime smacked against his sneaker, congealing to the side.

"What do you think you're doing?" The outraged cry came from Cass, who was struggling to her feet from behind the park bench. She glared at the new genner.

"Why, I'm saving you, fair lady." The snailman gave an awkward bow with a flourish of one meaty hand and a smack of his shell on the ground. "I recognize this man. He is Swipe. I am Snailman, and he is my archnemesis!"

She raised her eyebrows at Mick. "You have an archnemesis? That wasn't on the intake form."

"Because I don't," His actual enemies were his own business and not something a corporation needed to have on file. Especially since a particular corporation *was* his main archnemesis. He scowled at Snailman. "I don't even know who you are! I saw you for the first time when you were with the lineup of other hopeless heroes."

"Ah, because I have been too clever for you! I have been planning this for weeks, waiting for the opportune moment—for you to make your fatal error and fall prey to the wickedness of your ways." He stomped his foot on the ground for emphasis, sloughing through a pile of his own slime, which somehow didn't stick to him. If this confrontation didn't stop, people would notice, notify the police, and get out their stupid camera phones. "It is time to face a reckoning—"

Cass cleared her throat. "Speaking of face, that's a really interesting mask. Do you think it's the best choice for your bone structure?"

Mick knew that tone of voice. She'd used something similar debating assignments with teachers. Half the time she'd won through a mixture of logic and winsomeness.

"...what?" Snailman touched the green-brown mask, which had small eyeholes cut out in long swoops to allow his eye stalks to peer out the top. "I assumed so. I made it myself."

She shrugged and stepped forward. "I dunno. I think you could do better. The color isn't great either. It doesn't work with your skin tone."

"It doesn't? I wanted to match the shell."

"That's the problem." She sighed as if it were a terrible shame. "You shouldn't be matching. You should contrast—it will work a lot better on camera for daring escapades. The contrasting colors makes it look more dynamic."

He folded his arms. "Are you sure?"

"It's part of my job. I do branding and marketing, not just

publicity." She gestured to a nearby sign advertising Power-Up Publicity. "Calling me a publicist just means my bosses can pay me less."

Mick glanced at her. "And you still work for them?"

"Shut up."

"Make me." He couldn't help it. She was cute when she was annoyed. Especially now that he was so much taller than her.

"What are you, a two-year-old?" She whirled toward him, hands on her hips. "Don't make me come up there, beanstalk. And as for you"—Cass turned back to face Snailman— "He's my client. I'm a publicist who works with supervillains. It's my job. I'm not in any danger."

How had she managed to say that last line with a straight face?

Snailman's greenish mouth worked. "But ... he's a supervillain."

Mick snorted. "That whole classification is up for debate. People will pin a lot of labels on a man. Although if you keep slinging slime at me, it might push me over the edge."

It wouldn't. He would be long gone before that happened.

Snailman's eye stalks swiveled between the two of them for a moment. "You are infamous! I can't believe anything you say."

In the distance, people were looking their way, including a few cops on their lunch break. Of course, as a card-carrying hero—someone this sanctimonious was *definitely* registered in some database, even though Congress hadn't passed an official law yet—they'd buy the snailguy's story.

Mick's time here was up. He needed her answer.

He raced over to Cass. "Are you coming or not?"

She stared up at him. Trying to place his features? Perhaps. "Why are you doing this?"

"Not killing him? He doesn't deserve it. Not many do." Snailman didn't seem like the kind to really hurt anyone, even actual villains. Right now, his arm was mid-wave, bringing over the cops so local enforcement could feel special. What a slime-covered boy scout. "But as I said, I'm not doing that anymore. If I ever did." He leaned down. "Getting you out is the least I can do for an old friend. Unless you'd rather be cannon fodder."

"What if I do?"

Her gaze had turned calculating. There was the Cass he had known, always pushing boundaries. Testing how long she could last in a situation.

Then he pictured her back in that office with the heavy metal door. Almost resigned to the constant threat of supervillains. Almost expecting her eventual death.

Power-Up Publicity had hurt her. That didn't surprise him. The place was a cesspool of corporate stupidity and greed. He was going to take them down. But he needed to get Cass to safety first.

"I'd cart you off anyway before seeing you die in there."

The cops were closing in. Snailman inhaled, probably to hork up another pile of slime.

Was that a tiny bit of relief in her eyes? "Fine. But we do it my way."

He scooped her up in his arms, one hand under her knees and the other supporting her back. "What's that?"

"We do—"

Mick zoomed off down the street. Her words were lost in the movement, along with the scream undoubtedly in the back of her throat. Moving this fast was a lot for an ord, or even a genner who didn't have some kind of defense mechanism. One of the most effective ways to disable someone was simply to run them around a block or two. The human body just couldn't take it.

An instant later, they were inside his safe house on the eastern edge of the city. He turned away at normal speed, satisfied all the alarms were set and the door locked multiple times behind them.

"Are you going to put me down?"

He looked down at Cass. Not a strand of hair was out of place, and her face looked less pale than it should be. Or had been for others.

That was ... odd.

"You aren't sick?"

"No, although I'm really starting to miss those tacos." She sighed. "They smelled so good. So, the floor?"

Right. It had felt easy to carry her. Another weird moment, and not one he needed to think about right now. They had more important things to deal with.

Mick lowered her until her heels touched the concrete floor. Maybe she was just covering up her nausea.

"If you need to puke, bathroom's that way." He gestured to a brown door in a corner of the room.

"No thanks." She turned to scowl at him. "The ride wasn't bad—actually, it was fun, except for the bug that flew in my ear." She suddenly grinned. "By the way, you have a way to check for electronic bugs, right? Some kind of scanner?"

"A few, but do you really think they'd bug you?"

She shrugged. "Call it a hunch. Everything they do is off and has been since I started working there."

"They seem to treat you as expendable. Why bother with a bug?" Even so, he grabbed a few electronic wands, each of them keyed for a different listening or tracking device. Cass had always been suspicious about bugs, even in school—probably came from her off-the-grid parents. "Okay, this one catches all mech devices, this one will get anything the first one doesn't, and this one targets anything biological in your system."

"That should work for starters. No wands for you?"

"No way they got me bugged." He'd learned how to get around those a while ago.

"Okay, fine." She shivered, rubbing her arms as he waved the sensors up and down her body. Man, she might look similar to how she had in eighth grade, but she had definitely taken things up another level. And she had been a knockout then, even with braces and acne and ill-fitting, secondhand school uniforms. At least, he'd always thought so—it wasn't his fault that no one else had.

Not that she needed to know any of that.

As he finished, she rolled her shoulders back. "Thanks, Swipe. Or should I call you Mikey?"

He flinched, putting the wands away. "Mick."

"Aw, are you sure Mikey doesn't work? It always had a nice ring to it."

"Shut up, grill-marks."

Cass rolled her tongue over her teeth. "Not anymore." She glanced at the windows at the top of the white-painted cement walls. "Where are we? I couldn't really tell from the way over. A slum?"

He shook his head. "Slums often mean you're surrounded by criminals who want your turf or a payoff. No, this is a blue-collar neighborhood with workers from the local car plant and other factories. Salt-of-the-earth people who even have their own community watch. I'm on it as an occasional stand-in."

"Civic involvement? That sells, if you actually want to go hero, and that wasn't just a line to get me here."

"To safety. You're welcome."

"Oh, I'm grateful. Your growth spurt comes in handy." She turned around, reaching for something in her purse. "Did you toss my phone?"

"Miles ago, yeah."

Her shoulders sagged. "Good. They're definitely tracking it."

"I can get you a burner later if you need it." He tilted his head. "You're—"

"Not shrieking at you about my lost precious possessions? I guess I fail the damsel-in-distress criteria." Cass wrinkled her nose. "Don't worry, later I'll be sure to go out and buy food using my company credit card."

He chuckled. "That would cover it."

"I thought so."

"All your parents' skepticism of The Man helped out, huh?"

"Go figure." Her jaw worked. "After you lose your first coworker

... anyway, here I am. Alive. So that's something."

She looked away from him, taking in the room.

It wasn't much. There was no point investing in high-end stuff for a place he might abandon. Just a few cast-off brown area rugs from one of the factories, an oversized yellow couch, a minifridge, a futon in the corner, and a card table with one folding chair.

She walked over to the couch. "New? Or picked up off the street?"

"Try it and find out."

"I'll pass." She walked toward the chair.

He sped around her and sat in it first. "Couch is from a local outlet store. Certified floor model. Nothing gross."

She tilted her head. "And you're avoiding it because ...?"

"I like this chair." Plus, the card table had a pistol secured to the underside. He trusted Cass a bit more. Enough to bring her down here. But better that he be close to the firearms in case anyone invaded.

Or in case she was a mole after all.

Chapter Seven

She tilted her head askance. "So what happens now?"

"Now I use this"—in a split second he grabbed his laptop out of a secure location and returned to his chair— "to let my contacts know I need a fake ID and papers for you ASAP. Plus, I'll check in with some other connections."

Including texting Donny about this whole scenario and getting some clarity on whether he had meant for the intervention to happen, or if there was still more for Mick to do.

She nodded. "What do I do?"

"There's Chinese takeout in the minifridge. Enough for me, but I'll share because I'm nice."

"All right." Cass paused. "Hey, thanks. For trying to get me out. You're—it was a—" Her expression seemed to twist for a second into grief, anger. Amazement. A little fear.

Afraid of her company, or of him? It could be a bit of both. Maybe that was for the best. They didn't need to get too close again, even though she was fun to hang around. It was too risky.

"You're welcome."

A few agonizing moments later, three of the containers were next to him on the table, and one was on the couch next to Cassie.

She sat stiffly and paused for a moment, inhaling and exhaling.

Was she praying? Could be meditating. She'd always been skeptical of religious classes at Abundant Life Academy. He'd just taken all those classes as standard issue—church had been in his blood since birth, but it hadn't been for Cass. She'd been confused and irritated that her questions hadn't always been welcome.

It wasn't like he was that close to God himself. Enough that he'd stayed away from real villainy, enough that he'd reconciled ... he certainly wasn't pretty enough for the church crowd.

Not anymore, with his record.

Please let this be the right move. She could still be bugged without detection. Max Fields was always upgrading his tech. But here, there was enough shielding from the walls to block out major transmissions. Mick was lucky someone had decided renting out their vintage bunker basement was a good idea.

He scarfed down the contents of his containers, then pulled out his encrypted phone and texted his brother.

Went in. Came out with Cass. She the reason?

No answer. Well, Donny had other things to do too. Useless meetings. Press conferences to plan. Sick days to sleep through. Mick's heart twisted at the last thought. No, his brother was okay. He hadn't had an episode in months, at least.

Mick opened the laptop and started on the work, including contacting the accountant for some backup. If he was at a different safe house, he'd be able to do some of the work himself, but this one only had the basics. Besides, the White Coat's accountant owed him.

Every so often, he glanced at Cass. After the first hour, she'd kicked off her heels and curled up on the couch, flipping through a book she'd retrieved from her purse. A while later, she was leaning on the side of the couch, scribbling away in a notebook.

"Writing a book?"

"My last will and testament." She gave a crooked smile. "Journaling. When you have to try and keep your mouth shut every day, the words have to go somewhere."

"Makes sense."

"Don't worry, when I get to you, I'll be sure to mention your rippling muscles and dashing swagger."

He grunted. "Don't forget the way I swept you off your feet."

"And expected me to puke afterward. Yeah, that'll be there." She yawned. "How did you get powers, anyway? Which of the four culprits?"

"Four culprits?" His chest tightened. The question wasn't unreasonable, but that didn't mean he wanted to answer it.

He checked his phone again. Nothing from Donny.

She started ticking them off on her fingers. "Hereditary, making you a natural. Genetic experimentation, so a test tube. Damage from an accident. Random occurrence, which we all know isn't random, just recessive genes of a natural. So really, three culprits. Which of them is it?"

He cleared his throat. "Mixture."

"Oh?"

"I had the genes. Got a little help on them showing up." He started typing faster on his keyboard, letting the sound drown out the memory of the doctor looking at Mick like he was a freak of nature. Being led down the ornate hallway, scuffing the hardwood floors with the new shoes he'd been given. Facing the gentleman across the large, polished desk.

A man he'd never wanted to meet. At sixteen, he'd had enough with fathers for a lifetime. Especially after his dad had left Mick and his mom for a pharmacy clerk.

Bad things just kept coming.

Yeah, there were a few reasons why he hadn't filled a sanctuary chair or pew in a while.

"... Right. Um, what time is it?"

"Almost four."

"Hmmm." She stared up at the ceiling, tapping her pen on the notepad. "I don't suppose you have movies or video games? Maybe another book?"

Mick shrugged. "Not in this safe house. I've hacked a few streaming services on my laptop."

"The one you're using."

"To help you escape certain danger and death."

Cass nodded. "Well, later I'll have to introduce you to a few movies as part of your learn-to-be-charming education."

"Wait, what?"

"You're trying to become a superhero, right? At some point, you gotta do the work. Which should involve improving this lair. New paint on the walls, for one."

He harrumphed. "Thought that's why I pay you the big bucks."

"I'm not a painter. Or the one who has to speak to reporters and smile at the cameras. I mean, I can, but it won't mean as much. This is all about you, my friend."

Her friend? He paused over the words. After all this time, he supposed they still were. Enough that he was helping her, although that was partly thanks to Donny.

"I need to finish this up."

"Fine. I will take a nap out of sheer boredom—and gratitude to you, my daring villain savior who is scared of TV cameras."

"I didn't say that—"

She had already fallen asleep on the notebook, stretched out on the couch, somehow managing to fill most of it with her small frame. That ponytail was still perfectly in place with no flyaways. What was it, made of metal? Still, the purple looked nice against her olive skin.

Mick shook his head. He was helping her escape a bad situation that she wouldn't share details about, not dating her. No, that definitely wasn't an option.

The superhero stuff wasn't either. He already did his share of good deeds in his own way. Being in the shadows made it easier. Well, sometimes. Until the villains figured it out and came after him, which had happened. But he hadn't burned all his bridges yet.

He just wasn't the type, never mind how much Cass swore she could improve his image.

Why bother?

Mick sighed. Time to get back to work and get Cass out of here safely.

Chapter Eight

"Cass? Hey, Cass!"

Her eyes snapped open to stare at the blank gray ceiling above her. Not the ceiling of her apartment, nor of her office. Her heart thudded in her ears. *Where am I?*

A figure moved into her field of vision, and she turned toward it. Mikey Bruno—no, Mick Brown. That's what he went by now. At least it was an easy alias to keep track of, and considering how many Cassie had herself, she wasn't one to judge.

"How long was I out?" She rolled her neck back and forth, pushing herself to a seated position on the ... bed? No, couch. A couch in one of his safe houses.

"A few hours." He sat in a chair next to the sofa. "Feel better?"

The tone was blunt and dry, but it seemed like genuine concern showed in his eyes. She shrugged, stretching a little more to work out the aches and stiffness in her back. It did not like the couch or the lack of solid lumbar support. "Sort of? A bit. Getting fully rested isn't easy for me. But a Mountain Dew would fix that."

"Still an addict, huh?" He smirked.

"Hey, lately I'm drinking 'Dew Zero. So it's almost healthy. Everyone knows that green things are good for you."

He shook his head, a few errant strands of black hair falling into his eyes. "Whatever, Cass. I need a new name for your fake papers. Something you'll remember."

"Man, I'd gotten used to Robinson."

"Yeah, about that." Mick leaned back in his chair. "Why did you change it to Robinson? Did you have a falling out with your folks or something and ditched Royas out of spite?"

"Who says my real last name was Royas?" She slapped her fingers over her mouth. What was she doing? Augh, waking up with brain fog was the worst.

He blinked. "You mentioned your parents were off the grid, but that much?"

Might as well keep going along with it. "Yeah, Royas was a fake." She played with the tip of her ponytail.

"How is your hair still in place? Shellac?"

"Way too much hairspray." If she took the hair tie out, the hair would stay in place. A shower would feel good about now.

"Huh. The dye looks good. You talked about doing that back in school."

Cassie shook her head. "Not dye. A client had the ability to change hair and skin pigmentation permanently in themselves and others."

"That's a random power."

"Yeah, they were some kind of primal genner. It came from octopus or chameleon DNA or something—I think their test tube was also mixed with light power mojo. Anyway, after I helped them with an image makeover for a court appearance, they did the hair thing out of thanks." One of the rare moments that showed that maybe her supervillain clients weren't completely evil.

"So, if you're not Royas, what's your actual name?"

Beam. Cassandra Liwanag Beam. Her father's last name and her mother's maiden name for the middle. Letting herself *think* the truth had always made it easier to avoid *saying* the truth. At least in her head, she was being honest. "Mick, I'm glad you're helping me, but it's been thirteen years and I don't even know where you've been—"

He sat up abruptly. "Fine. Smart, in fact. So, what do you want as a new name?"

"Give me a second. If I don't have my Dew, it's going to take my brain a bit longer to kick into gear." Cassie tapped her fingers against the side of the couch, letting her mind wander. It was best for brainstorming. "So, you know if you go hero, you'll need a new handle as well as a new look."

Mick sneered. "I'm not turning hero. No tights or gelled hair."

"Good grief, not everyone does that! Besides, your hair doesn't need gel. Also, we're talking a lot about hair right now. Let's change the subject. What about clothing? Maybe a more aerodynamic suit to go even faster?"

He shook his head. "Not interested. I'm plenty fast."

The blank look on his face piqued her curiosity. "How do you know?"

"I know."

"But how—"

Police sirens blared through her words. Mick cursed and leaped to his feet, eyes fixed on the red-and-blue flashing lights through the tiny windows near the top of one wall.

Fear cut through her meandering brain.

Cassie threw on her heels and stuffed her notebook into her purse. Meanwhile, Mick rushed around the bunker—or at least, she assumed he was, because things kept happening. The bathroom exploded in flames, and a metal door slammed over it. The laptop disappeared somewhere. The couch and futon were shoved into a corner and doused with some kind of chemical.

All of this happened in the span of maybe thirty seconds. Then he stood in front of her, a backpack slung over his shoulder.

"We have to go."

"Come out, infamous Swipe!" A familiar nasal voice blasted over a bullhorn.

She brushed off her blazer. "Or we could just have a nice talk with Snailman and get him to see reason."

"Won't work. He's already decided I'm a villain."

"Whose fault is that?" Cassie threw up her hands. Why couldn't he see that he was making this worse for himself? Granted, the current situation wasn't ideal.

"Cass—"

"You can't keep running forever, Mick."

He glared at her. "It's worked so far. You wouldn't understand."

Cass held up her hands, fingers splayed. "Ten. I lived in ten different places over the course of eighteen years. Were your parents paranoid about government takeover 24/7? Did you go to school under an alias? I don't think so."

Her parents were still paranoid. It was one of many reasons why she hadn't had contact with them in years. But that was also a reason to track them down, because they could hide her. Maybe even more than Mick could, since this safe house had just been discovered. Which meant that she needed to use Katrina.

Mick sucked in a breath. "We need to go. Now."

"Fine. But this time, we're going to Katrina."

"Katrina?" He shook his head. "No outsiders—"

"She isn't an outsider. Kat has stood by me when no one else did." Cassie grinned. "She even let me stay with her through my college years."

Mick frowned. "Why are you grinning?"

"It's my face. I like to grin sometimes." Especially when the inside joke was this good. After the events of the day, she could use a bit of fun.

"You know, I could just sweep you up and force you to come with me."

Sirens sounded again.

"Come out, Swipe!"

Cassie's stomach dropped. Maybe Power-Up Publicity would get involved. Would they track her down, or dismiss her escape as a lost cause? If it was the former, she couldn't go back. Not when she was so close to freedom.

She stepped toward Mick, daring to place a hand on his arm. "Come on, Mick. Please. We tried it your way, and we were found out somehow."

"I have other safe houses."

"I have Katrina. I promise you, we'll be out of here."

Mick sighed. "If you had this escape all along, why not use it before now?"

"I didn't think I'd be able to get to her safely." She squeezed his arm, feeling the warm skin and corded muscle beneath. "Please? You have to admit, I have way more experience avoiding the feds than even you do."

Come on, please. He had to listen to her. Katrina was a lifeline. A chance for Cassie to finally break out.

His jaw worked, and his muscles tightened beneath her fingers. "Where is this Katrina?"

Cassie rattled off the address, a place outside the city, then gave his arm a final squeeze before releasing. "Thanks."

"Sure." The single word was as curt as his expression. "Let's go."

They probably left out the back entrance. She couldn't really tell with how fast Mick was going. Earlier she had been able to get a little bearing on their surroundings. Now everything was a blur, although her stomach was just fine. If anything, the increased speed was even more exhilarating than the first time.

After what seemed like moments—and probably was—they stood in a junkyard outside the city. Old washing machines, broken down trucks, and various messed up paraphernalia lay in haphazard piles. The air smelled of rancid oil and mildew.

Her heart thudded in her chest. This was it. She was finally here, and suddenly filled with energy, like she'd already downed a Mountain Dew.

Mick glanced down at her, his breath soft in her face. "Some home. Where is this friend of yours?"

Cassie jabbed a finger at a van in the far corner.

"She lives in that rust bucket?"

"Sort of." Cassie gave him a winsome look. "You already brought me here. No backing out now."

He sped off, and a second later set her down next to the van. It had originally been white, but mud and what looked like rust stains pockmarked the surface. "Looked like" being the operative phrase. The decals had taken forever to paint.

Cassie strode toward the side, narrowing her eyes. "Where is that spot ... aha!" Then she turned to Mick. "You're not photosensitive, right?"

"To what, strobe lights?"

"Something like that. Only they're advanced sensors."

"What? Where is Katrina?"

"This is Katrina. Katrina Van Tassel." *The Legend of Sleepy Hollow* had always been a favorite short story. She pressed her hand just to the right of one rust stain. "Hopefully this still works."

After all, Kat had been here for a year all alone. The owner of the junkyard had been well paid, but that didn't mean anything. Who knew what abuse her baby had gone through?

Silence.

"This is a waste of time," Mick snarled. "We need to get out of here."

"One more minute."

"So the cops can pull out some of their genners and sic them on us? So that *snail* can finally catch up?"

"One. Minute."

She pushed her hand more firmly into the panel. She had set the highest level of security before leaving Katrina here. It might take a bit longer to get her van going again.

After a few more seconds, a sound like electric eggbeaters started up. Cassie exhaled. Good. Kat was still alive.

Bright white-and-silvery-green sensors flared out from the top of the van, bathing them in biometric scans, along with a few others that she didn't entirely understand.

One beam focused on Mick's shoe and beeped.

"Tracking threat detected," intoned a neutral female voice.

"Take off your shoe," Cassie said.

"What?"

"Your shoe! It's a beacon, somehow."

Mick studied the shoe. "The only thing there is slime ... wait. No." He gritted his teeth. "That stupid snail slime. He can track it."

He pulled out a knife and started cutting away at the material. Cassie turned back to the lights. All of them were now fixed on her.

"Bio-threat detected."

"Where, Kat?"

"Systemic. Neutralization in process."

Her pulse jumped. What neutralization? She hadn't seen that feature on any schematics.

What had her parents done to her van? It had to be their idea.

A bright red beam blasted out from the van, coating Cassie

in light. It pierced through her clothing, stinging through every pore in her skin and setting her veins on fire. She whimpered and squinched her eyes shut, trying not to fall to her knees and pass out.

The pain stopped as suddenly as it had started.

"Threat neutralized. You may enter the vehicle."

"Thanks. What was the threat?"

"Advanced biological identification agent. Purpose unknown."

"Great." Cassie swiped a hand across her forehead, then reached for the side door handle. She looked back at Mick. "If you really want to go, I can take it from here."

He stared back at her. "You still don't have new IDs."

"I can figure something out."

"No. I said I would help, and I will." The genner looked over her van in disbelief. "Besides, you need to explain how the heck your family created something like this."

"Doesn't everyone have gap-year projects?" Cassie winked at him, then slid back the door. Somehow, she felt a bit lighter knowing he was sticking it out with her, even though it was just duty and loyalty. Maybe she was just seriously lacking friends. "Get in, then. As you said, we don't have much time—"

Sirens blared in the distance.

A chill ran down Cassie's spine.

"New threat imminent," Katrina intoned.

"No kidding," Mick grunted. "Let's go, Cass."

She scrambled inside, pushing through the separating curtain and easing into the driver's seat. He dropped into the passenger bucket seat next to her.

"The windows are crap," he muttered.

"Thanks, Captain Obvious." Cassie shoved her key into the ignition and turned, hoping against hope that the solar cells still worked.

After a few sputters, the engine started rumbling. Her shoulders loosened slightly, but there was no time for relief. The windows might be grimy, but she could see flashing red-and-blue lights through them well enough. At least there were no flying heroes around. They were the top-dollar contractor genners. So were the energy ones, especially if they were naturals.

"Cass, now!"

"I know!" She smashed her foot on the gas pedal and swung around the nearest pile of rubble. "Not helping."

The van bumped over potholes and crunched through debris. There were several outlets from the junkyard. She needed to choose the right one.

"Kat, guidance for a safe exit."

"Optimizing." A few seconds. "Route found. Veer left."

Mick glanced over his shoulder. "A GPS? Where's the screen?"

"Didn't get it installed before I left for college. Audio only."

"Great."

Cassie focused on the dirt road in front of her, skidding around a wreckage of washing machines. One of the exits loomed ahead of them, just a half mile away. "Good job, Kat."

Something thudded and crinkled from the back of the van.

Her heart clenched. "Mick, what's that?"

"Projectile assault on the rear of the vehicle," the AI explained.

"No duh!"

Cassie gunned the engine. Katrina could go pretty fast, but she wasn't built for speed. She had other perks. "What is it?"

"Grappling hook." Mick opened his door. "Or something like it. Probably a strength genner trying to force us to stop."

"Augh, no!"

"I got it. You're not even going that fast."

The speedometer was over seventy-five, but it probably was nothing to the speedster.

"Mick, be safe—"

The door slammed shut.

She swallowed hard and focused on the road ahead of her. Mick knew what he was doing. Sure, in middle school he had been in the back of every gym class, but he was clearly a different man now. There was nothing to worry about.

Another smash and a crunch of metal.

"Stop it!" She didn't even want to think about the bodywork poor Kat would need.

"Projectile assault on the rear of the vehicle," the AI intoned.

"I know, girl. Just give me a little more juice."

The entrance loomed. Beyond that was a thicket of trees and a state highway. Good. They could speed down the two-lane highway and disappear in small towns for a bit. The GPS might be audio only, but it still worked.

Something banged into the front door.

Cassie shrieked and roared through the exit.

"Hello to you too." Mick's voice was rough with sarcasm—and exhaustion. "All clear. Bozo wasn't even much of a fight. All weight lifting and no agility."

"No one else?"

She swerved onto the state highway with a screech of tires.

"Someone with water powers, but that was useless in a dry junkyard. Not much ambient moisture for them to pull from."

"Good." Cassie stole a glance at him. Her friend had sagged back in the seat, clutching his shoulder. "You okay?"

"I'll live. Faster healing from the metabolism." He yawned, and blood trickled down the side of his face. "Barely an inconvenience. Just a bit of ringing and lightheadedness."

"Yeah, concussions are chill like that." Cassie shook her head. "There's a small first aid kit in the glove compartment. No falling asleep on me."

Out of her periphery, she saw his lips tilt up slightly. "On you? Was that an option?"

"Nope. You wish."

"*You* wish."

She grinned despite everything. All she had to do was keep Mick talking a bit longer, get in an hour or so on the road, and then she would check him out.

In a completely platonic, he'd-better-not-die way.

CHAPTER NINE

Something was burning.

It was the first thing Mick noticed in the darkness. The scents were cinnamon and a stench like too-hot metal.

He wrinkled his nose.

"Come on, it wasn't in *that* long!"

His lips twitched involuntarily. That frustrated tone was all too familiar.

"What, you don't like your toast blackened to a crisp?"

"Steak, sure but—oh, you're awake."

"Looks like it." Mick rubbed his eyes, then opened them and eased into a seated position. He was leaning on a pile of assorted pillows on top of a mattress covered with a yellow sheet. A surprisingly big, comfortable bed. His legs were stretched out, and the side of the van was still a few inches away.

"Is this a full mattress?"

"A queen, actually. Which is why it takes up all the space. It's a special order for my back." Cassie glanced over him from where she was poking forlornly at a piece of burnt toast. "You asked the same question when you were about to pass out, but I understand why you wouldn't remember. I'm just glad you managed to make it to the bed at all."

He nodded, taking in more of the interior. The bed took up the rear of the vehicle. There was wood paneling along the walls and inset lighting strips, along with built-in shelving and a small flat-screen TV on a swing-out stand. Next to the bed was a narrow pathway with a counter along one side that featured a small sink, a one-burner cooktop, and mismatched cabinets above and below, plus the tiny toaster oven. On the other side were more cabinets and a sliding door. Maybe a shower?

"Checking out Katrina?" Cassie abandoned her plate of dead toast to walk over and sit on the edge of the bed. "She's held up pretty well, even though I had to abandon her. I've been giving her some TLC while you rested."

He focused on her again. She wore sweatpants and a gray hoodie, and her dark purple hair lay damp down her shoulders. All her makeup was gone, leaving her face clean and open. Nice to look at. "How long was I out?"

"Four or five hours." She gestured to the darkness outside the window. "I was worried, but you assured me that sleeping while concussed wasn't bad for you. So after I settled you back here, I drove a while more, got us out of Missouri and on the other side of Indianapolis. Then I stopped for some groceries, clothes, backup diesel, and supplies, and found this old campground. Since then, I've done an oil change, checked the fluids, that sort of thing."

"And took a shower?"

She snorted. "Yeah, they have a shower house. I still need to deal with the gray and black water tanks before we'll have running water here. But there's a spigot outside."

Warm admiration flowed through him. "You seem to know this van well."

"I should!" Cassie gave him a light shove. "I helped build her, after all. Although my parents are both geniuses. They helped. But they insisted I be part of everything, since she's my ride."

He stared at her.

"What? Surprised? I mean, there are also seven giant binders filled with procedures. I don't keep all this stuff in my head. I just followed the manuals."

"Still, this is really impressive." Mick held her gaze. "You held out on me when we were kids."

Cassie shrugged, playing with a lock of hair. "Well, you were a fifth-generation Christian schoolboy with a grandparent on the board and an aunt teaching chemistry. I was an off-the-grid, outcast atheist stuck going there because of reasons."

"What were those reasons?"

She paused for a moment. "I guess that's not a huge secret. My Filipina grandma was very Catholic. She left a trust fund to my parents, but to claim it, they had to send me to a Christian school for three years. My Lola preferred a Catholic school, but the will said any Christian school would do."

"They needed the money for ...?"

"My scoliosis. I needed surgery, remember?" Her fingers traveled to the spine pendant around her neck. "We didn't have insurance—mostly, we didn't need it. My folks arranged for medical visits in their own special way. But I was always the problem child."

She kicked her legs up on the bed next to him, grabbed a few pillows, and stuck them behind her back.

"Right, that's why you left." He remembered the fear in her eyes behind her sarcastic remarks and bravado. The surgeon had been a genner using experimental new methods with their powers. But her scoliosis had been getting worse at the end, enough to interfere with other parts of her body.

"That's why you gave me this." Cassie held out the pendant with a small smile.

"I can't believe you still have it."

"Yeah, I mean, a Christian gave it to me. That meant good blessing vibes, right? I was scared, and well, that's all it meant then. That and ... you were my closest friend."

Her quiet admission left him silent. He tried to find the words that would give voice to the odd tightening in his chest and the sudden urge to reach across the space between them and pull her closer.

"Well, it's held up good for a cheap gift." Mick cleared his throat. "You wearing it was one of the tip-offs that made me think I could trust you."

That and Donny's message. Had this been his idea all along? Mick needed to check his phone for texts when he had some space.

His friend's smile widened. "Right, because you're some dangerous supervillain now. So you thought maybe I'd gone evil too?"

"I didn't go evil. I just ..." Found out some special things about his family tree. Nope, this wasn't the time to bring that up. "I'm figuring that out." He exhaled in a long gust. "Things happened after you left."

"Apparently. You'll have to catch me up sometime soon." She leaned up and swung her legs off the side of the bed. "For now, I need to check your bandages, and then you need to eat."

As if on cue, his stomach growled. All of that healing had done a number on him. "Sounds good."

She moved toward him, reaching for the bandages across his forehead. This close, he could see the faint pebbling of acne scars and something more serious. Thin white lines, indentations from above her cheekbone and down to her lips, like something with four claws had raked them across the right side of her face.

"Good news! That genner metabolism did what it was supposed to." Cassie pulled away the rest of the bandages and reached for a clean rag. "Just wipe your face with this and you should be fine."

He took the rag from her, catching her hand for a second. "Cass, what happened to your face?"

"Well, when one is cursed with endless zits at thirteen and can't resist popping a few—"

"Not that. The four parallel scars."

Her brown eyes darkened. "You catch me up on how you're a villain with powers who happened to be at Power-Up Publicity for some unknown reason, and I'll share about my beauty marks."

Mick opened his mouth to protest, but his stomach growled louder.

"For now, food. Then you can give your excuses—" She yawned.

"Until I fall asleep. Which will be happening soon."

Chapter Ten

Food turned out to be a pile of sub sandwiches crammed into the small fridge, packages of cookies, and the option of bottled water or sodas. After he'd demolished two foot-long sandwiches, three bottles of water, and a Dr. Pepper, Cassie handed him a pile of clothes, shoes, a bar of soap, and a towel.

"I had to guess at sizes, but after all that running, you need to change. The shower house is that way." She nodded to a small cement building with a metal roof and outdoor lights illuminating the darkness around it. "It's not bad, just watch out for the spiderwebs."

Mick rifled through the clothes. "No credit card, right?"

"Oh yes, and while I'm at it, I'm posting videos of our escape on social media." She rolled her eyes and shoved the clothes into his hands. "I have my stashes of cash."

"That rhymes."

"Go! Before you smell up Katrina permanently."

"It's not that bad."

Cass shook her head. "Says the man who clearly lives alone. It wasn't bad after the first super-speed run. After the second and third—well, I have the windows cracked for a reason. And Kat has a good ventilation system. We'll be driving for a while. Go."

"Still bossing me around."

"Only because I want you around, but I also value my nose."
She cleared her throat. "I mean, it's nice having someone around
to talk to who isn't trying to harm me or use me or seduce me or
all three or—"

Mick smirked. "Right. Got it."

Cass was even more cute flustered now than when they were
younger. She wet her lips in the same way and shifted from side
to side. Even though she was shorter now, she still had the same
presence.

She had to. People were trying to hurt her. He strode into the
shower house, flipping a switch for an ancient fluorescent light,
which immediately attracted a cluster of flying insects. A knot
tightened in his stomach. Someone or something *had* hurt her.
Those marks looked like some kind of claws. And those were only
the visible scars.

Not again. Not if he could help it.

He might not be interested in the official hero stuff—not that
he hadn't done the right things when he could, but he didn't need
the gold star and labels for it. He could do fine on his own.

But he wasn't going to let Cass walk back into that deathtrap.
At least, not alone. Maybe she would find her parents and decide
to stay there, but Mick doubted that. She'd already mentioned her
commitment to helping heroes. Knowing how stubborn Cass was,
that probably wasn't going away.

Inside the shower house, he checked his encrypted phone for

anything from Donny. One message. He opened it.

Yes!! She's important. Go with her. And then a fireworks emoji and a thumbs up and a smiley face because clearly those were important to the message.

Why? Not that Mick minded the job, but what was the big picture here?

An ellipsis signaling a response. He stared at the screen.

The three little dots disappeared.

Nothing.

A groan escaped him. Ten years, and the kid still just disappeared at inconvenient times. Even with Donny's business responsibilities, this was ridiculous.

Unless he was in danger.

Mick shook his head. His brother would have told him. Probably with a few screaming emojis. *Well, no point in waiting around.*

After a quick wash-up, he got into the clothes which fit decently enough. The shoes were his exact size. A good thing because his last pair had been almost worn out, and that was before he'd had to cut out the slime-ruined patch.

A final check on the phone. Still nothing.

Cass was throwing away a small bag of trash in a metal can when he returned to the van. She eyed him. "Glad to see the shirt fits."

"Why MIT?"

She shrugged. "My dad gave it to me to use as a sleepshirt. I like oversized shirts, and I think maybe he was hoping it would inspire me to achieve my potential."

"They wanted you to become a computer nerd?"

"Something like that. My parents both went to MIT." Cass scrunched up her face and shoved her hands into the pockets of her hoodie. "By the time I was eighteen, my fifteen-year-old sister was in her second year at Johns Hopkins in some kind of premed track. Meanwhile, I took a gap year to build Katrina and ... figure out life, I guess. My parents kept waiting for me to have some insight or revelation—atheist version of divine guidance? Not sure." She shrugged. "Anyway, I never wore the shirt, so you might as well. Weren't you into robotics and stuff?"

He nodded, pushing away the faint, dumb disappointment that the shirt was new instead of worn by her. "For a bit. Things changed in high school."

"Yeah, we need to catch up on a lot of stuff." Cass slid open the side door and sat down at the edge. In front of her was a tiny fire table. She set the coals ablaze with a fire starter. "Come on, have a seat. Katrina has good anti-spy tech stuff, but it only works close to the van."

"Fine, but only if there's marshmallows." He sat next to her, because hey, he needed the calories. He didn't like talking to people much, but she wasn't a person. She was Cass.

"Uh, yeah. My IQ might only be 120, but I'm smart enough to figure that out." She pulled out two long metal forks and a bag of jumbo marshmallows. "Come on, for old time's sake? We used to do this at the edge of the sports field, remember?"

Mick laughed and grabbed a few. "Your parents still harped on your 'slowness' after you left, huh?"

"Yeah, it was back to homeschooling mixed with online classes. They didn't always talk about it specifically, but I could see they were discouraged. Sometimes frustrated. Sometimes yelling." She poked her marshmallows into the flames until they caught fire. "Sometimes ... my fault."

He nudged her. "Failed things on purpose?"

"Once in a while. Maybe more than that. When they look at you as if a B- or C+ is a failure, then why not actually fail? Didn't do that in college, though. I had to keep that minimum 3.0. Even managed a 3.2. Got a 165 on the LSAT. Didn't matter after I dropped out, of course."

"Because of hero worship."

"Hey, the Emergence had just happened. Everything is still hot with genners going official. The laws are being made right now. New online video channels are still popping up, heroes are being open about what they do, society is all over the place—it's where I wanted to help. Especially after the doc saved my life." She popped a marshmallow into her mouth and chewed slowly. "The pain got really bad just before the surgery. Even with the brace all the time, my spine just kept moving and ... all kinds of symptoms. The doc essentially broke my spine, then using her healing powers, put it back together."

Mick whistled. "You managed to find a regen genner? I thought all of those were grabbed by gangs or rich people or something." Some people expected them to work until they keeled over—like it was a moral imperative.

"She was on the run from some people. All the money we paid

71

made it so she could disappear to another country. I have no idea where. But even after she left, whoever was after her smeared her name through the press, making up crimes and accusations." Cass set her jaw. "She saved my life. She was this ... this miracle from God, and that's how they treated her. That's why I wanted to go into law at first, and then marketing. Court of law or court of public opinion. Somewhere I could push back against the bullies and help real heroes." Cass faltered. "Then I got tricked into helping supervillains."

He patted her on the back, silently thankful that she had survived. That she was alive and here with him. "Okay, that sucks." Mick stared into the flames, working over what she'd said. Cass had gone through some serious crap. He guessed ... he could give her something in return about his powers. Nothing huge—after her confessions about only wanting to help heroes, the last thing he wanted to do was share some of the garbage he'd done or the mess Donny was in—but something.

"My powers might be killing me."

Chapter Eleven

"What?" The word came out way too loud, judging by how Mick grimaced.

"You dropped your stick."

"What? Oh." She grabbed it off the ground and brushed some dead leaves off the sticky end. "What do you mean your powers are—is it because you're a test-tube genner?"

"Yeah, something like that."

Her hands played uselessly with the stick, trying to process the information. This couldn't be real. They'd just found each other again. Not that their escape meant they were destined to be together, but this just wasn't fair. "But how?"

"As I said, recessive gene. I already had latent speedster powers. Who knows? Maybe they would have shown up later. But I was a pissed-off teenager, so I did something drastic."

Cassie gently placed her hand on his arm and squeezed. "I'm sorry."

"Don't be. It was my stupid fault and stupid choice. Turns out the serum I got pushed everything into high gear. One of the gangs I was in had this high-level scientist who checked out the new recruits for kicks. And his boss ... turned out to be very interested in the results." Mick stared into the flames. "There's cellular decay every time I use my powers. Not much, but it adds up and gets worse when I go at top speed, so I usually don't."

His words spun through her head. "So you're dying?"

"Everyone's dying. Someone's dead right now." He shot her a grim smile. "And right now, and right now, and—"

"Okay, shut up you morbid jerk." She shoved him and scooched away with a shiver, pushing away all her memories of the last eight months.

He snorted. "That was one of *your* jokes back in the day."

"Yeah, well, people change. I've seen too much death and been too close to it to make it funny anymore."

"Makes sense." Mick shrugged. "But it really doesn't mean anything for me, since I don't know when I'm going to die anyway. The most the scientist could say was that I'm losing some of my potential lifespan, whatever that is. I never think that far ahead. I'll die when I die, and considering what I do, it'll probably be way sooner than that potential ending."

Cassie glared at the ground in front of her, her insides turning and twisting around at this news. At the cold, hard words coming from the man next to her. A man who remembered the same friendship as her, but now was different. Like she was different.

Right, a test-tube genner. I wonder ... The question flew out of her mouth. Maybe it wasn't the right time, but she had to know. "What kind of test tubes?"

"What?"

"Your serum. Was it synthesized from existing genner DNA or

from animal DNA?"

Those were the two options for test-tube powers. If his abilities were mental or elemental, then Cassie would know they were from natural genner DNA because that was the only origin, at least as far as the latest public research. But physical enhancements could also come from a synthesis of animal DNA. They were the most unstable genners.

She stroked the scarred right side of her face. Mick hadn't shown any signs. Still, she had to know.

"Genner DNA."

Cassie slumped down. "Okay."

At least there was that. Granted, there were the problematic ethics of where the original genner DNA had come from, and from whom it had come. But that was the lesser of two evils, at least for her.

"Why do you ask?"

She paused. The words caught in her throat. Too soon. It was too soon.

"Just curious." She flipped a lock of hair over her shoulder. "So this is why you didn't want an aerodynamic super suit, huh?"

"Sure. Also, it would look stupid."

"You haven't even seen any concepts!" She stuck her tongue out at him.

Mick grinned. "Doesn't matter. It's still stupid."

Cassie opened her mouth to protest, but a massive yawn escaped instead. Her limbs suddenly felt like lead, with a side of achiness. "All right, time to sleep."

She got up and doused the fire pit with several nearby buckets of water, then picked up the fire table, her muscles straining. Stronger arms took it from her and moved it inside to an empty space under a counter.

"Only one bed, huh?"

"No. I have some bedding that fits in the hallway between the counter and the shower. It's a tight fit, but—"

"I've slept in worse places," he finished quickly.

"Good." She yawned again. "Ten hours, and then we're back on the road."

Mick slid the door closed. "Ten hours? I thought we were trying to get somewhere fast."

"Ten hours. I need them."

"I could drive the first leg while you sleep—"

"No intruders may take command of this vehicle," the AI intoned sternly.

Cassie rolled her eyes. Typical Katrina. The van's overprotectiveness was comforting after almost a year away. "She's right. It has to be me, and I have to get that sleep to hope to stay awake."

"But you also slept this afternoon."

"It's a hobby of mine, I guess. It always has been, you remember?" She tilted her head at the ceiling. "Kat, enable locking protocols, activate self-defense systems, and enable perimeter alerts."

"Affirmative."

"Thanks."

As soon as she managed to get up and energized the next morning with 'Dew—and Mick had washed all the windows for safety reasons—they were on the road. They stopped for a drive-through breakfast, then Mick played DJ for a while between different stations as they drove through backroads. He still wasn't a morning person, and she didn't mind singing along by herself when the mood struck her.

After a brief lunch stop, they entered a span of Ohio with gently rolling hillsides and small leaves on the trees. She entered fresh coordinates into the GPS and pulled onto the main highway. Cassie would've preferred the backroads, but this was the most direct way. Hopefully no one was following them now. They were out of police jurisdiction, and maybe Snailman was local to St. Louis. Local independent heroes didn't have the funds or manpower to chase someone out of state.

Cassie rubbed her eyes. They'd get to the checkpoint soon. She really needed a nap, even with the Mountain Dew.

"Power-Up Publicity is the premier company for your genner career. Whether hero or villain—"

"No. Please."

Mick had already shut off the station. She glanced at him and smiled.

"Thanks. I don't need any more reminders."

"Yeah, definitely," he grunted. "So, why were there police after us?"

"Because they wanted to catch us. I can do that logic."

Mick growled a little in his throat. "Yes, but why you?"

"Who says they were after me?" She shrugged uneasily. "You're the villain. I'm just the bystander you grabbed."

"Do you really think it's just about me?"

Unease shivered down her spine. Cassie forced a chuckle. "Snailman did say you were his archnemesis. Very impressive and somehow poetic. You know, because you're really fast and—"

"I get it."

She sighed, finally letting herself consider all the possibilities she'd been pushing away. "Maybe Power-Up Publicity doesn't want me going to the press with how badly they treat their employees?" Her fingers tapped the steering wheel. "They made me sign a ton of NDAs. Not that I care about those, but something isn't right about the company."

"You have no idea," he muttered.

"And you do?"

"I mean, I think I do. I was there to investigate what they might be up to in the supervillain publicist area. I got a tip from ... a friend."

"Another supervillain?"

"A colleague. Donny."

Cassie took a swig of soda, then frowned. "What kind of tip?"

"He just said I should investigate." Out of her peripheral vision, she saw Mick shrug. "He's ... an inside man."

"But he isn't a supervillain."

Mick scoffed. "Not any more than I am. Way less."

"Yeah, that clears things up." Cassie shook her head. She wasn't going to push him about this guy. It wasn't like she was being open about her family situation. Time to change the subject. "Well, I don't know why the company would be after me. I'm not a genner. I'm not even a genius." She gave another short laugh. It was impossible. It had to be—she was past the age that powers showed up. "Maybe they're impressed I survived when my coworkers kept dying or mysteriously disappearing."

Mick gave her a sharp look. "How did you survive?"

Gosh, why did he keep asking questions? "I don't know. Like I said, no powers. But I've definitely gotten injured."

"They didn't experiment on you? Give you anything in a serum?"

"Why bother?" Her voice sharpened. "If Power-Up Publicity wanted to start an illegal experimentation wing, there are plenty of people willing to pay them money to go under the knife. They could increase their profit margin and have willing guinea pigs." She gave Mick a quick glare. He scowled back at her. "This isn't helping, Mick. Just chill out."

Cassie threw on a pop mix station and cranked up the music, letting the familiar melodies and fluffy lyrics drown out her thoughts. Or at least, she tried to. Despite everything, her mind couldn't help but toy with what he'd said.

After stopping at a rest area, Mick caught her hand before she could turn the ignition. His voice was flat and serious. "You are one of the few people I've carried at super-speed who didn't at least get dizzy."

"So I have some genetic quirk of anti-dizziness. I'll become a professional roller coaster test-rider." She shook off his hand and revved up Katrina, pulling out into the parking lot.

"Have you always had good equilibrium?"

"I don't know. I do like roller coasters, but I haven't gone to an amusement park in a long time." What was he saying? That her lack of reaction meant something? It couldn't. It was just a coincidence. She turned onto a two-lane road just as the sun was starting to get lower in the west. "Okay, we're getting close to the checkpoint."

His shoulders tensed. "What is this checkpoint?"

"A safe place to meet up with family." Her parents had her memorize all of the locations when she was younger, then they'd input them into Katrina's database. Hopefully both were still accurate.

"More family than just your parents?"

She turned down another street, past another farm, and through a partly wooded area. "Oh yeah. The off-the-grid paranoia runs pretty deep. Some of my relatives find jobs that let them work in the middle of nowhere. Others go into developing countries with less surveillance. My sister's been doing humanitarian doctor work overseas."

Cass pulled onto a gravel road. After a few miles, she drove into an abandoned gas station lot, complete with broken-down pumps and the shells of a few cars.

"We have arrived," Katrina intoned.

"You never asked questions about this?"

"It's not illegal, Mick." She drove into a parking space with faded white lines, pushed a button on the dashboard, then turned off the van. "My parents were very open about distrusting the government and valuing self-sufficiency. They never hid anything from me about their reasons. It was odd, compared to a lot of people—I learned that when I went to your school—but odd is a matter of degree anyway."

What was Mick trying to get at? That her parents or family were somehow special? Cassie considered the idea. Maybe it would explain their obsession to stay off the grid. But her parents would have told her about something that big, if only for utilitarian reasons. Because as they said, ignorance was the doorway to stupidity.

He glanced around, barely able to make out the small convenience store in the light of the full moon through the trees. "So, we just wait here?"

"Yup. I gave the signal. We'll see if they're nearby." Cassie unbuckled her seat belt and stretched. "Meanwhile, I'm going to take a nap."

"After all that soda? It's not even dusk yet."

"Like I showed you back at the safe house, I can sleep when I'm bored, even with caffeine. It's like a part of me is always waiting for a nap." She yawned. Maybe she could forget about what he'd said. Naps were good for that as well. Then a relative would arrive and they would take the next steps, whatever those were. It would work out. "Feel free to stand guard if you want. Katrina has self-defense mechanisms, but I'm sure a speedster can always help."

She squeezed his shoulder, then walked back through the curtain to the rear of the van. "Katrina, activate self-defense systems and implement familial identification protocol."

"Activation confirmed. Would you like to activate the closed-door protocol as well?"

Cassie poked her head through the curtain. "Nah, Mick can leave if he wants. He's not a prisoner."

Mick rolled . "Nice of you."

"Yeah, I'm sweet like that." She wrinkled her nose at him. "Although Kat apparently has a few surprises that even I didn't know about, like the biochemical neutralizing agent from earlier, so hopefully if you leave, you can get back in."

"Hopefully?"

"My parents are protective. They helped build Katrina. So getting locked out could happen." She sighed, giving him a smile. "Look, I know all of this family weirdness is a lot for you. My parents are good people. They'll have answers to whatever questions we have."

"Because they're family." His voice had an edge of mockery. "They'd never lie to you. Families never break those close to them."

Anger flared within Cassie. Her family might have attitudes about their IQs and might have been tough on her, but they loved her.

When she spoke, she let her voice get a bit softer. Colder. "Because I've worked for villains for almost a year. I know the difference. Good night, Mick."

CHAPTER TWELVE

She ducked back behind the curtain. He could hear her thudding toward the bed. For someone so short, she moved like a tiny elephant.

Mick scowled, staring out into the woods. Her belief in her parents made no sense. He had reconciled to a higher power worthy of trust. But people were another matter. Even if they professed faith in something, it didn't necessarily mean anything. His high school years had proven that.

And parents could be the worst to trust. Especially in Mick's case, when one of those parents had far too much power and apparently enough interest in Cassie that Donny had noticed and sent Mick in. At least, that's what he could deduce at this point.

He kicked up his feet on the dashboard. An ambush was only a matter of time.

"Inappropriate action taken. Potential injury to vehicle structure."

"Cass did this earlier."

"Invalid response." Did the AI sound smug? "Cease your hostile action against this vehicle."

Mick rolled his eyes. Definitely smug.

"Fine."

He dropped his shoes off the dashboard and moved around in the seat, trying to find a comfortable position. The seat wasn't built for someone over six feet tall. He found a button to tilt it back, which was marginally better.

Too bad he hadn't brought a book with him. When Cass woke up, he'd ask her where she kept her stash. There seemed to be a million hidden storage compartments in the van. At least a few had to be mini libraries. She'd been reading at the safe house, so she must still enjoy it.

Something flickered out of the corner of his eye.

He turned toward it, staring out the side window.

Nothing.

Mick's pulse kicked up. He knew that kind of flickering—an invisibility power being used. If an invisibility genner wasn't careful, their movement could just be visible, at least to his eyes.

They'd been followed.

He bolted for the back of the van where a small shape was curled up in a heavy-duty sleeping bag.

"Cass, come on. We need to go. Now."

"Mmph." The lump rolled over, a mop of purple hair falling out one side. Brown eyes blinked up at him in the dim lighting. "I'm ... Kat is safe."

Darn it, she was cute, and this was not the time to think about that. "Not right now. There's at least one genner outside, maybe two, and she hasn't flagged them."

"Two?" Cass rose up on the bed, shoving down the sleeping

bag and settling her hoodie into place. "Kat, are there any threats outside?"

"Negative. No threats in the immediate vicinity."

"Define immediate vicinity."

"There are no threats within one hundred feet of the vehicle."

Cass turned to him. "Kat's sensors are really good. She even considers flu germs a threat."

Mick grimaced. Was he really going to be overturned by the AI again?

"What if one of the genners has tech powers?"

She finished pulling herself out of the sleeping bag and grabbed her sneakers. "Okay, that's fair. I'm not sure my parents considered genners much when we built this. Other than the surgeon who did my scoliosis procedure, we never had contact with any other genners."

"Anti-genner?"

"No, just cautious. Cautious about everyone, like I said." She threw her hair into a messy ponytail with pieces falling around her face. "So what's the plan? Take on at least two genners? Run off into the woods?"

"No threats in the immediate vicinity," the AI repeated pointedly.

Mick groaned softly. The arrogant metal beast could shut up any day now. "Do you have a bug-out bag in here?"

She gave him a look as if he'd asked her about having a brain. "Of course. Except for my time at Power-Up Publicity, I've always had one around."

"Grab that, and we'll make a run for it. I can get us to the gas station ten miles back before I'll need a rest."

"And you'll need all of their protein bars as well." She glanced around the van, running her fingertips along the wood paneling. Her expression seemed wistful. "Are you sure?"

A deep voice boomed from outside the van, as if through a bullhorn. "We know you're in there, supervillain. Come out with your hostage. Now!"

Her gaze hardened. "Not happening." Cass knelt, grabbed a canvas bag from a compartment under the bed, and slung it over her shoulder. Then she grabbed his hand. "Let's go."

Her skin was cool to the touch even though she was bundled in sweats and had just come out of a sleeping bag. Did she ever get warm?

Mick squeezed her hand, then dropped it and moved toward the center of the van in front of the sliding door. He scooped her up into his arms, the edge of her ponytail tickling his cheek. "Hold on and enjoy the ride."

"Just go already." She swatted him lightly. "Kat, upon our exit, go into shutdown. If anyone attempts to break in, initiate defense protocols."

"No threats in the immediate vicinity—"

"That's an order."

He zoomed out of the van, the world seeming to flow around him at breathtakingly slow speeds. This was Mick's element. A place where no one and nothing could catch him. Nothing could hurt. Everything was calm, even quiet. Cass's heartbeat in his arms was a gentle metronome lullaby—

Something hard and invisible smashed into them, as if he had run into a giant, impermeable windowpane. Shock and pain jolted through him. The faintest beginnings of a cry emanated from Cass, so slight to his speed-heightened senses.

Adapt.

Go.

Get away. Now.

He turned to the right to get around the forcefield—another smash—to the left—

Mick fell to his knees, out of the calm speed and into harsh reality. Searing brightness blinded him. He narrowed his eyes. Some kind of energy power turned into material constructs?

Cass twitched in his arms. "What's going on?"

"Stay behind me." He set her on the ground and rose instantly to his feet, his speed powers accelerating his healing.

"We have you surrounded, supervillain. Surrender the hostage, and you will not be hurt any further."

"Still think no one is after you?" he muttered.

Behind him, she snorted. "I didn't say you were wrong. I *implied* you had bad arguments about why." Then she spoke louder. "Who are you? Why do you care about me?"

"You are a captive who must be freed. We're under orders."

With the last word, a blinding bolt of energy blasted out from the light. Mick gritted his teeth as it burned through him. He'd healed from worse, but that didn't make it fun. Especially when it would take more days off his life to heal.

"Mick!"

"Cass, stay behind me."

"Surrender the hostage—"

"The hostage is fine! Also, *I'm not a hostage!*"

Another blast of energy ripped through him, the agony of the solar current cascading through every part of his body.

A guttural yell escaped him, and wetness streaked from his eyes. Every part of him was focused on endurance. He had to survive this. No matter what.

"You have clearly been brainwashed. You'll understand afterward."

Blast number three arced toward them.

Mick braced himself.

"No!"

A much smaller shadow darted around him and into the light. His mouth dropped open.

Cass, you idiot!

Never mind their discussion earlier. As far as they both knew, she was an ord.

The blast might kill her.

Chapter Thirteen

This was insane. She was going to die.

Why had she run out in front of Mick? Was a gut instinct worth it?

As the light blinded her, all Cassie could think was, *I'm so stupid.*

Definitely not the best parting words before heading up to heaven.

"Cass, what are you doing?" Mick's words were a fierce whisper above her.

"Dying, probably?"

"I think you're failing."

Why did he sound so ... shocked?

Also, why wasn't she in pain?

Cassie cracked her eyes open. The light was still there, but instead of killing her it flickered around her skin. Whenever it came close, it seemed to blur and fade away.

"What's going on?"

The brightness around her intensified. But it only seemed to give her more energy. For the first time since she'd left the van, she was warm. Energized. Like she'd downed five Mountain Dews.

"Dumb woman," the genner scoffed. "So much for bringing you

in uninjured."

Something in her reared up at the dismissal. It echoed Flaze in her office. It echoed every single contemptuous supervillain who hadn't even wanted to try and be better, to do better. Why should they? They had power and money to pay someone to pick up the pieces after their bloody, evil escapades.

And she wasn't dead. Which meant the gut instinct was right—and so was Mick. There was something special about her. She had a power.

God, let it be something useful. Besides the fact that it was keeping her alive.

"How about you get injured?" she snarled.

"Cass—"

"I've got this, Mick." She strode forward into the light. One step, then another, letting the energy flow around her and into the core of her being and bones.

Voices shouted at the edges of her vision. Maybe they wanted her to stop. Maybe they were angry that they were losing whatever bounty or bonus they would have gotten. It didn't matter to her.

"Go. AWAY!"

With that, something intangible flared off her body, throwing all the built-up energy outward in a wave of power. Releasing every bit of anger and hurt she'd swallowed over the last eight months.

The light suddenly disappeared. So did the warmth.

Cassie blinked and folded her shaking arms across her chest. In the faint light of the moon, she could see three bodies around her. Unconscious. Or so she hoped.

"Oh crap." What had she done?

"*Now* you decide to be badass?" The words were low and fatigued.

She whirled around to see Mick falling to his knees.

"Crap, crap, crap!" She ran over to him, coming alongside him and taking his muscled arm. "Did that hurt you? I'm sorry, I didn't know what I was doing—"

"I knew there had to be a reason they were after you." Even in the feeble light, his smirk was as clear as the smugness in his tone. "Why your parents were on the run."

There came the 'I told you so.'

She swatted his shoulder. "Jerk. You aren't that smart."

"I'm smart enough." He groaned. "Also, I could use a hand to get back to the van."

"Since there's no one around to see you look less than awesome." Cassie used what remaining strength she had to be his crutch. Slowly, they moved toward the sliding door. "Wouldn't want to hurt your burgeoning superhero reputation."

He grunted. "Not a hero."

"Not yet. But you're getting there." She patted his arm, then surveyed the prone bodies. "Should we just leave them?"

"No choice. I don't think you can dead lift them, and bringing the bodies along is suicidal."

Cassie made a face. Mick was right. "Katrina, open the side door."

"Complying."

After the door slid open, she let Mick boost off her shoulder into the van. As he gripped the countertop and made his way back to the bed, she pulled out her burner phone.

One quick call to 911. Then she threw the phone to the ground, closed the door, and made her way to the driver's seat. Good thing she'd bought more than one phone.

"Kat, let's get out of here."

Hopefully she had enough energy to get them a little bit farther.

With a screech of the tires, she maneuvered the van away from the abandoned gas station and back onto the open road. Her fingers gripped the steering wheel, knuckles white as she tried to stop her hands from shaking.

"Deep breaths, Cassie. Just take deep breaths." She should've grabbed a blanket before getting into the driver's seat. Everything seemed hot and cold at once.

"Cassandra, you appear to be physically damaged."

"I'm fine, Kat."

"You are impaired." The AI was using her bossy tone.

"Impaired? Maybe you should check your external sensors before you go accusing me, all right?"

The van's voice fell silent, leaving Cassie to her thoughts. Her mind immediately went back to the showdown.

What had happened back there? What had she done?

She had powers, but it couldn't be powers. Powers emerged around puberty, or at the latest by age twenty-two, even in guys who tended to mature a bit later. She was twenty-six.

"Late-bloomer doesn't cover it." A hysterical giggle escaped her, and the road blurred for a second. She swiped away tears. Had someone experimented on her? Had her parents lied? "What is going on with me, Kat?"

"I am occupied with sensor analysis." The AI's tone was frosty. "It appears the malfunction was not the result of a technological intrusion."

"Maybe some kind of cloaking power shielding the baddies?"

The AI was silent for a moment. "It is possible."

"Mmhmm." Another burst of giggles escaped her as she stared out into the night. "Look at all the lines on the road, Kat. So wiggly. Squiggly and wiggly—"

A blast of cold air hit her. Cassie yelped. The road came into sharp focus. "What was that for?"

"You insist on driving impaired," Kat answered primly.

"We have to get away from the checkpoint! Mick is out cold on the bed. Who else is going to drive?" She felt around the front console. "Where is my Mountain Dew?"

"I can implement the autopilot function."

Her fingers paused on their way to the plastic bottle. "What autopilot function?"

"The autopilot function your parents installed in this vehicle."

"They did no such thing! They would have told me ..." She grabbed the bottle and unscrewed the cap. "This was our project. Together."

Her other hand slipped from the steering wheel as her stomach twisted. This couldn't be happening. It couldn't be real. Mom and Dad wouldn't install something on the van without telling her.

Except they already had. Her traitorous brain reminded her of the extra-special scan she'd endured a day earlier before Katrina would let her in the van. She hadn't approved that scanner.

"Implementing autopilot function."

In front of her, the wheel started moving on its own, keeping the van perfectly between the lines on the road. Much better than she had done.

Cassie fell back against the seat. "Lookit you, being all driverly."

That wasn't even a word. She knew that, but it really didn't matter at this point.

"You are impaired. Rest is required."

"I can sleep here. Very comfy." She yawned and swigged the Mountain Dew. It wouldn't keep her awake at this point.

"The seat you are in is suboptimal." Kat affected a motherly tone. Cassie's actual mother had programmed special subroutines into the computer, after all.

"What will people think if they see a van driving with no driver in the seat?" Her head bobbed forward. "See? I can think. I am smart. Maybe not as smart as some people ... kinda dumb compared to Anda, but—ouch!"

Her seat warmers had kicked up to scalding. She flinched up.

"A holographic projection will be sufficient. You must depart to an optimal resting place."

"Augh. Fine, you meanie." Cassie stuck her tongue out at the steering wheel. She should be questioning this more. But it was hard to string even a single thought together.

Somehow she managed to get through the curtain to the middle part of the van, then onto the bed. Mick had sprawled over a lot of it, but there was space for her on the side closest to the sliding door. Mostly because she was small. But he was flopped on her sleeping bag.

She sighed and grabbed at it half-heartedly. The gray-and-silver fabric didn't budge.

"Always have a backup. That's what they say."

Grabbing her spare out of a compartment, she rolled up in it, then flopped across the edge of the bed with her back to Mick, enjoying the security of his presence next to her. Right now, she needed to not feel alone.

"Hard to"—she yawned— "hard to feel alone with Kat."

"It is my duty to serve you, Cassandra."

"I love you too."

Her eyes slipped shut, finally giving in to exhaustion.

What seemed like a moment later, something bright lit up behind her eyelids.

CHAPTER FOURTEEN

It can't already be morning. Cassie groaned, rolled over in her sleeping bag—and came nose-to-elbow with a tanned arm flung across the bed, because apparently six-foot-whatever Mick was making himself comfortable again. Still, a big difference from middle school, especially across the shoulders and, well, the chest and—

And I probably should stop noticing him like that. He was sleeping, after all, and staring was creepy. *I will not be a creeper.*

Especially because Mick was still a supervillain of some kind. One who hadn't told her anything about how he'd become one or how he'd gotten his powers. In other words, fun to be around—at least so far—but not someone to get in any deeper with than she already had.

She rolled back over, scooching up and down with her knees until she reached the edge of the bed, wincing a bit at her sore back muscles. She hadn't managed to find her knee pillow before going to sleep.

A yawn sounded from behind her. "Do you have a second secret power as a caterpillar?"

"Maybe as an inch worm." She unzipped the sleeping bag and

threw it back in a corner of the bed.

"That one." He yawned again. As Cassie glanced over at him, Mick pushed up with his palms until he was sitting up and leaning against the cabinet headboard. He pushed back his black hair with one hand, staring at her with dark, piercing eyes.

Her breath shallowed. *Get over it. Still just Mick. The dork who shoved straws up his nose after you dared him.*

True friendship. She raised her eyebrows. "What? Why are you staring?"

"Oh, your hair. It looks like you stuck your finger in a light socket."

"Augh, really?" Cassie patted down the frizzy dark purple strands, then gave up. "I forgot to buy more smoothing spray at the store yesterday. Too busy trying to get supplies for Katrina and food for you." She pushed at a small panel in the wall and pulled out several protein bars. "Here, you'll need to refuel to keep healing after that energy blast."

She threw the bars at her friend, who caught them deftly, then added two water bottles. He blinked, his eyes unfocused for a second as if picturing something else. Then his gaze focused on her again in a glare.

"You ran out in front of me like an idiot."

"I didn't die, though." Cassie gave him a quick grin, hopping up on one of the counters. She started swinging her legs out and back, tapping them lightly against a cabinet drawer. Suddenly she was ready to run a marathon—and also, lightheaded enough to pass out. Both were true right now.

Mick guzzled down half a bottle of water before responding. "You didn't know you wouldn't. It was still a dumb move." He took a bite of energy bar, chewed quickly, then swallowed. "I was protecting you."

"For how long? Until you keeled over from too many energy burns? Then they would have taken me anyway." The words came out sharper, and her heels tapped a staccato rhythm on the plywood.

"I could have outlasted them."

"Liar. I was behind you. Your healing isn't that fast." She dropped off the counter, putting her hands on her hips. Why was he lecturing her when his plan hadn't been any better?

He balled up a protein bar wrapper and threw it at the built-in shelves on the opposite side of the van. "What were you thinking, Cass?"

"I ... I wasn't, all right? You proved it. I don't think sometimes, I just operate on gut instinct. It's the reason I left with you, *by the way*. Happy?"

"Why would I be happy? You could have died!"

"I didn't! I'm fine."

Mick glared at her. "You didn't know you'd be okay."

"Yeah, but I had an idea, especially after all that talk with you in the van. It wasn't completely reckless." Just mostly reckless. "Why do you care?"

He opened his mouth, then shut it with a mulish look.

"This is the third time you've escaped with me, Mick. The third time you've protected me. Why?"

"Old time's sake."

"You're that nostalgic?"

Mick threw away another protein bar wrapper. "Why are you asking this question now?"

"Why not? I don't know, after all. Except that you just couldn't leave me there because we were old friends. But that was *one* rescue. Why the other two?"

His expression turned blank. *Was* Mick her friend? How well did she really know him? She knew his criminal record and some details about why he was at Power-Up Publicity. That was all. She had done most of the talking and sharing, as usual. She had filled in all the details, and after the initial skepticism, had jumped right into looking after him as if they were on the same team. She had even poured out her life story. He'd just shared about his powers a bit.

Was she being stupid? Impulsive?

"You know what else I don't know?" She ticked the phrase off on one finger and kept going, fire heating her gut. "Why you ran away from home—because I'm assuming you did? Why you ended up as a supervillain. And why you've stuck around *when I have Katrina.*"

"She missed the villains last night," he bit out.

"You had foreknowledge of that, hmmm? I guess you have a second superpower too." Cassie shook her head, the staticky ends of her bangs floating in front of her eyes. "I guess I shouldn't expect you to tell me anything. After all, we were friends thirteen years ago. You don't owe me anything, not even a straight answer." She pressed her lips together. "I just thought—"

I thought I could trust you. But Mick being a human barricade wasn't enough. Maybe once she would have liked to be swept off her feet like that, but not now. Even though his powers were breathtaking and set her veins on fire. And darn it, she really, really liked having a friend. Someone she didn't have to be careful around. Maybe that was her mistake.

He had to have an agenda.

Still, he was bigger than her. Stronger. Faster. All she had was a weird, undefined ability. Even if she wanted to kick him out, she couldn't. Katrina might be able to, but that was the last option, because the AI's methods tended to be very final. Besides, Mick was still healing. It would be unfair to throw him out now. Maybe after she'd eaten some breakfast and gotten her head on straight, she could think of something. Right now, it took everything to hold back her tears.

"What did you think, Cass?" His words were even.

"Never mind. Just rest up back here. Help yourself to more food, if you want."

She turned and walked toward the front of the van. Along the way she grabbed a hair tie and yanked her hair back into a low ponytail. A shower would be good too, but she still needed to deal with the tank situations. "Kat, where are we?"

"A Wal-Mart parking lot in Centre County, Pennsylvania."

"Good." The department store was open about allowing RVs, and her van was close enough. She checked the dashboard clock as she sat down in the driver's seat. "How is it three in the afternoon?"

"It is a fact that the use of superpowers takes a toll on the user."

"I don't even know if these are superpowers. Or what's going on with them." Cassie held out her hands as if she could somehow see through her pores and into her DNA. A question rose in her mind, one that she was almost scared to hear the answer to. "Kat, do you know if anyone else in my family line is a genner?"

"Unknown." The word was flat and tinny.

Her heart clenched. "Not 'no.' Are you sure?"

"Unknown."

She tried a different tactic. "Is there anything in my genes that predisposes me to genner characteristics?"

"Unknown."

"But you *should* know, because you literally scanned my body before letting me on. It's a legitimate question."

"Unknown."

Cassie sighed. "Great. There's a lot you don't know."

That wasn't suspicious at all. Her parents had already programmed an autopilot function into her van and a special scanner. As much as she hated to admit it, it was likely they were behind Kat's sudden ignorance on a topic that Cassie wouldn't have even thought to ask about twenty-four hours ago.

Her stomach growled. Absently, she pulled a packet of chocolate sandwich cookies out of a side compartment. They were a bit stale, but they were food.

She could almost feel Kat's disapproval. "Your body requires more suitable nutrients."

"Why would it? After all, I'm just an ord, right?"

"That is unknown."

"Why is it unknown?"

No answer from the AI. Cassie slouched back in the seat. Thankfully the parking lot was huge and had a corner with a cluster of trees. It was much more pleasant to stare at them than at random shoppers walking by. Although she usually enjoyed people-watching. But that was before her entire life upended. Before she had chewed out the guy who had, in fact, taken energy beams for her. A guy that she had trusted more than was reasonable.

She reached for the bottle of Mountain Dew. As her fingers closed around the plastic, the sound of plodding footsteps knotted her stomach. Apparently Mick didn't have his speed back all the way.

"After thirteen years, I'm surprised your blood isn't pure Mountain Dew."

She continued staring out the windshield. "Who says it isn't?"

"You should ask Kat to scan you again."

"She would just say, 'Unknown.'" Cassie swigged the soda, then made a face. Of course, it would be flat. She dropped it back in the cup holder. "I'm not speaking to you, by the way."

"Clearly." The bucket seat next to her squeaked as he settled into it.

She shifted positions. If only she still had a smart phone to play a game on. Hmmm, there was still the journal in her purse. Cassie pulled it out, along with a pen, and turned to a fresh page, clicked the pen, and started a sentence.

Really early this morning, I discovered I had— She tapped the pen on the paper. Had what, exactly? It hadn't manifested again. She didn't seem to have any sort of special perception or anything like that. *I don't know. I was somehow able to absorb powers or ... deflect them or ...*

The pen trailed off on a line across the page. She sent up a silent prayer for clarity and answers about herself or what she was meant to do next in this situation. It was better than being at Power-Up Publicity, but as it turned out, escaping from the heinous firm hadn't solved all her problems.

"Augh."

"What?"

She shook her head and turned in her seat, staring out at a different tree. Mick wasn't getting her to talk. Although why he would want to was beyond her, since he didn't really care what she had to say except to make her feel dumb. She could have just left the van, but it was *her* van!

He sighed. "...I'm sorry."

"What?" Cassie turned in her seat to face him, eyes narrowed. "What do you mean?"

Mick's lip curved in a faint smile. "You know what the word means."

"I haven't heard it in a while from anyone. At least, not in a genuine way." Without thinking, she touched the four scars on her right cheek.

"Right." He winced. "They really beat you up in there. The supervillains."

"You do know you're still one of them, right?"

He scowled. "In name only."

"I saw your record, remember?" She bit her lip. "Was every crime altruistic?"

"That would be impossible." His words were dismissive.

Then she would tell him something he couldn't throw aside. "I got these scars my first day on the job. I hadn't even finished settling into my office when he came in."

"Who?"

"I don't know. He wasn't my client. But he was a supervillain who stopped by to 'break me in.' To let me know who was boss." She fiddled with her pen. "He was taller, stronger, had faster reflexes, and claws from some kind of animal gene splicing experiment. And when I tried to deflect his attention, to get him to leave, he grabbed me by the throat, shoved me against the wall, and gave me these scars. Marking me as his."

"A primal." Mick muttered a curse. "Test tube animal synth. That's why you asked me about my power origins."

"Yeah." Cassie took a breath, then continued. "The only reason he didn't go further was that my actual client came in and killed him with an ice blast to the back. Not to rescue me. She just didn't like that he was taking up her appointment time."

His scowl turned hard. Earnest. "Cass, I'm not like them."

"You can say that all you want. But there is something to branding. You wear the name supervillain, you hang around supervillains, and you play by your own rules and justice. Is that right?"

His jaw worked. "I was doing fine."

"Of course you were." She tensed, ready to turn in her seat once more.

"Just because someone appears to be a *hero* doesn't mean anything." He spat out the words. "Talk to my dad about that. If you can find him."

"What about him?" Mick's dad had been something important in the church. Cassie couldn't remember the title.

Now it was his turn to stare out the windshield. "He decided that the woman he'd been having an affair with for years was more important than his own family. We were holding him back. I was fifteen."

Her heart tightened. "Oh, that sucks."

"We had to leave the area."

"Wasn't all your family in that area?"

"Back three generations on my dad's side, and at the school too. Every friend I'd ever had." Grief flashed in his eyes. "Mom couldn't take all the gossip and rumors. I tried to pull a brave face, but ... it got to me too, how quickly everyone turned their backs. We ended up settling closer to her side of the family, but after that, she didn't trust them either, so they were still an hour away. We had no one."

That had been one of their big differences. Her family never put down roots, whereas his had gone deep. She remembered how he'd relied on that community, even when he acted like it was annoying.

Instinctively, Cassie reached for his hand across the gap between seats and squeezed. "I'm really sorry."

He shrugged. "I'm sorry I asked all sorts of questions about you and avoided talking about myself. I'm not used to sharing."

"Well, thanks." She pushed her bangs out of her face. "I guess it was nice to start to trust someone. To not be alone against the world."

"I don't mind being alone now. It's safer, but—" He paused. "You're you. Although it seems like I didn't know you as well as I thought I did."

"I told you everything I could. You knew my parents were different. You knew everyone in my family were geniuses."

"I didn't know the degree." Mick tapped the side of the van.

A clipped alert sounded. "Cease the hostile attack, intruder."

"Calm down, Kat." Cassie rolled her eyes. Despite everything, her muscles relaxed back into the seat. "Yeah, we don't really know each other that well."

"Still, you kept the necklace."

"...Yeah." She rubbed the spine pendant.

His expression turned thoughtful. "You should see something." Mick started pulling down on the collar of his shirt.

Her cheeks heated. "Whoa, what? Um, no thanks."

"Relax, it's just a little bit. I'll try not to be insulted that you aren't excited about seeing me with my shirt off."

"Life is hard for speedsters."

"We're a persecuted people." Now a small section of his skin was bare. "Come on, look a bit closer."

She shouldn't, yet curiosity would not be denied. Cassie leaned forward. Her lips parted in shock.

"Is that ... a spine tattoo?" It was. A small one, about the size of her pendant. It was on his chest about the same place where the pendant rested on hers. "Where—why did you get that?"

"After I got powers and joined a gang."

Her brow wrinkled as her fingers reached out to lightly stroke the mark. "You didn't have to get the same mark as everyone else?"

"It was a stupid gang. They couldn't decide on a symbol. So I got this." His voice was rough. "I guess I couldn't think of anything better."

Cassie tilted her head up to look into his eyes. His face was close enough now that she could feel his breath on her cheek. Yet there was no urge to pull back. If anything, she wanted to lean in closer. "Right, because there are no other symbols or shapes or marks in the world."

"Obviously not."

"You're such a liar."

He lightly traced the edge of her jaw. "No, I'm a strategic user of information."

"Uh-huh."

She absolutely shouldn't climb into his lap and kiss him right now. They had just admitted they barely knew each other. They should be talking more. This was not a smart idea.

His hand drifted up, fingers teasing the shell of her ear before moving down her neck. Heat flowed through her.

Strike that. His lips definitely looked like a smart idea.

A klaxon blared through the van. Cassie yelped, falling backward. Strong arms grabbed her and pulled her into a standing position.

"Alert. Federal agents imminent. Alert."

Mick swore. "The feds?"

Cassie threw up her hands. "I have no idea how. This van is supposed to be off the grid."

"It's failing so far."

"You keep saying that." She moved into the driver's seat and turned on the van. "Kat, ETA?"

"Imminent."

Chapter Fifteen

"Imminent?" Mick repeated, smacking his fist into the side door as three unmarked cars zoomed into the parking lot. "Thanks for nothing."

The feds had the worst timing. Thirteen years later, and he'd finally gotten *that* close to Cass's lips. Not that it was important right now.

"Hostile attack—"

"Kat, shut it." Cass sped through the parking lot. "I'm sorry, she hasn't had a system upgrade in years."

By now the cars were flanking them. Two of them easily sped up to match and exceed the campervan. Mick swore again. He might be able to take out the tires of the two in front, but it wouldn't help with the flankers. As much as he hated to admit it, he still wasn't at a hundred percent. Going over seventy miles an hour would be a stretch.

Cass swerved around an empty area of the parking lot. "Ideas?"

"Does this crate have any weapons?"

"No, of course not."

He shot her a look, and she shrugged helplessly. "Not that I'm aware of. Mom and Dad aren't that violent."

"As far as you know."

She glared at him. "Watch it, Mick."

"I'm just saying—Cass, look ahead!"

"What?" Cassie squinted through the windshield, then her jaw dropped. "No way."

Snailman was leaning out a side window of one of the cars, his hands extended. Mick groaned. This couldn't be happening.

A second later, globs of slime shot out from Snailman's palms, coating the ground in front of the van.

"Crap!" Cass slammed the brakes. "Kat, emergency stop measures!"

"Affirmative."

A moment later, the van screeched to a stop, but not before the front tires were completely covered in slime and stuck fast to the pavement. Mick winced. He didn't like Katrina, but no one deserved that pile of mucous.

Cass yanked her key out of the ignition. "What now?"

"Now we get out of here as fast as possible."

She turned in the seat toward him, eyes flashing. "Leave Kat in the hands of the government?"

"Better than *us* in the hands of the government!"

"Maybe I can make some kind of bargain."

"You think they'll go easy on a supervillain publicist?"

Her mouth opened to respond, but a tapping sound emerged instead. Mick blinked. It wasn't from her. Someone stood at the driver's side window. A federal agent, if her tight bun of black hair and serious face were to judge. There was also the badge she was holding out.

Crap. He pulled out his phone and tapped a tiny button on the side. An upgrade he had insisted on, even though Donny hadn't understood the need. Thankfully, the criminal underworld had better tech than the feds, at least in this area. And that underworld included Max Fields's private R&D department.

The device began to heat from within, as if it were self-destructing via tiny microwave. Which was sort of what was happening. He threw it on the floor of the vehicle. Even when it was found, it would be useless. As long as the tech held up.

Cassie twisted back in the seat. "Anda?"

She rolled down the window.

The woman's thin lips twitched slightly. In her other hand she held a taser. "Special Agent Andrea Garvey. I am taking both of you and this vehicle into custody."

"Anda, what the heck are you doing working for the government? You're supposed to be in Bangladesh."

Electricity flashed from the taser, jolting through Cassie. Her head lolled to the side and her body sagged down.

Mick's heart clenched. He grabbed for her, but his movements were agonizingly slow. Before he could reach Cassie, the agent had opened the door and caught her, then slammed the door in his face.

He lunged after her, calling on all the speed he could muster—but something like fast-drying concrete held his shoes in place.

"Aha, we meet again!" It could only be one person. "I knew you could not escape justice, villain. Nor could you succeed in kidnapping that innocent woman."

"I didn't force her to come along."

"No, but perhaps you coerced her with your sinister, seductive wiles."

"You've got to be kidding me!"

Anger flared within him as he turned in his seat. That arrogant snail had chosen the wrong time to get sanctimonious.

Then volts of electricity shot through Mick like a million tiny bees crawling beneath his skin. He jerked in his seat, muscles loose, healing factor a distant wish. All he could think was that when he came to, that hero would get punched right in the eye stalks.

The pain disappeared into darkness.

When he awoke, Mick lay on a cot in a plain cell. His body still throbbed faintly.

Cass. Where's Cass? As he sat up, his movements were slow. He hadn't eaten enough for his healing to fully kick into gear. He cracked his neck and rolled his shoulders back and forth.

The room was empty and cold. No sign of a clear exit. Just gray cinderblock walls, fluorescent lights embedded in the ceiling, and the cot. He glanced at the ceiling corners. There must be security cameras hidden somewhere.

No point in asking about Cass. They wouldn't tell him, and it would only reveal his feelings, which was definitely not a good idea.

We'd been so close. The brief memory of their almost-kiss flashed through his mind. Why hadn't he just gone for it? Because she'd gone through a lot of crap and wasn't in the most stable place. So he'd stayed respectful. Careful. Except then they'd been grabbed by the feds at the worst possible time.

His stomach growled. Speaking of bad timing.

"No food or water? So much for humane government treatment."

Something like a bright spark flashed in the middle of the room, causing Mick to shield his eyes. When he opened them, a bottle of water and two protein bars were on the floor.

"So, you have a teleporter somewhere," he muttered. "Of course, this means I have to trust that the stuff isn't drugged."

He looked around the room again. Could the person in charge be baited into giving something away? It was worth finding out. Slowly, he stood up and walked toward the fuel. "I was in a lot of gangs, but you know, they say the government is the worst because they hide behind self-righteous laws."

"The food has not been tampered with."

There was the familiar resonant, nasal voice. He reached down and carefully picked up the bottled water and protein bars with exaggerated caution. "I dunno. Maybe you slimed them."

A huff sounded over the unseen speaker. "I should have, but I am a *hero*. We heroes do what is good, even to our enemies."

"I didn't hurt you, even when I could have. Both times." Mick strolled back to his cot. It wasn't like he could go anywhere else. "Am I a villain?"

"Your record speaks for itself."

"My record contains half the facts. You're not including motives or what actually happened."

There was silence from Snailman. Meanwhile, Mick ravenously consumed a protein bar. It tasted like compressed cardboard, but his muscles immediately thanked him. Heightened metabolisms sucked sometimes.

"You might have a point. Theoretically."

Mick flicked off a disrespectful salute, then chugged the bottled water. "You're too kind."

"But even if your motives were pure, theoretically, if others do not know them, then they can't be blamed for treating you like a villain."

"They could just leave me alone."

"If you really wanted to be left alone, why are you intervening in public affairs?"

He paused, second protein bar in hand. "I'm not. I'm just stopping bad stuff when I see it."

"You're stopping others. You're assisting the public. And the public is governed by laws."

"That's not my problem."

"Yet if you are helping others in your own way, you trust the laws to protect those people. You trust the emergency rooms to care for them, or social services to assist them."

"So?" What was the snail guy getting at?

"You're trying to play both sides, Mr. Swipe. You want the freedom to do whatever you feel like at any given moment. Acts of villainy one day, acts of heroism the next. When you choose to act the hero, you rely on the systems you disdain to help those you rescue. When you act the villain, others should simply understand that you really don't mean it and leave you alone rather than exacting justice based on your actions. Do you expect the world to revolve around you, or that everyone else should be telepaths to read your intentions?"

"I don't expect ..." He gritted his teeth.

Damn it, the hero couldn't have a point. Not about the public relations stuff or the communicating-with-others garbage. Trusting others only led to pain. Especially when it meant trusting the so-called good guys. They always failed.

An image of his dad with his girlfriend surfaced in Mick's mind. The man who had taught him right and wrong, who had taught him about responsibility, who had led Bible studies, now trying to claim that he had found himself. The rest of the world just had to understand and let him follow true happiness. The fact that it had split their church, made Mick a pariah—or a target for trite sympathy—and forced their move had only made things worse.

Speaking of worse. An image of Max Fields flashed in his mind, the day he had summoned Mick to his office after Mick's transformation with the serum. When Mick had learned the rest of the truth about his past.

What would Cass think if she knew? He'd have to tell her if he ever saw her again. Better for her to know before she let her feelings get ahead of her brain. He might not be a real villain anymore, but his connections ... that was another story.

With that realization, his appetite was gone. He set the

remainder of his protein bar aside. Better to hang on to it in case Snailman didn't give him more.

Mick searched for a rebuttal. "How do you know the good things I did?"

Another bright spark flashed in the room. Snailman stood there, dressed in some kind of gray uniform without insignia. It looked less comic book and more military casual-confused. His narrow, pinched face looked slightly superior to match his voice, which was a weird contrast with the eye stalks. "You're skilled at subterfuge, Swipe, but we have our own resources."

"Is that so?" Mick eyed him up. Maybe he could rush the hero, but what good would that do? Snailman could just spew slime at him. Besides, Mick was getting tired of running at this point.

"In addition, our department received an anonymous file of information. Our IT specialists vetted and decoded it. It turns out your claims are correct. You have committed a number of altruistic acts over the last few years."

Huh. Had the anonymous file been Donny? His half-brother was decent at tech, but not that good. Mick sat back on the cot and leaned against the wall. "Don't sound so disappointed."

"I'm not. Only ..." Snailman sighed, picking at the webbing between his fingers. "Our team leader is considering your situation for future work."

"What?" The word came out as an explosion. "You grabbed me and Cass off the street like a pair of criminals!"

"Ms. Robinson is not considered a criminal. As for you, apparently allowances can be made if you're willing to offer information and eschew your life of villainy."

"But aren't you my archnemesis?" Mick smirked.

The snailman appeared to be gritting his teeth. "I made that up because I wanted a defined target. You have no idea how hard it is to even confirm villains or heroes when the laws are so shaky right now. Also, it seemed fitting with your powers."

"Because I'm your opposite. Got it." Mick worked their conversation over in his mind. This was ridiculous. He couldn't be considering joining the hero crowd.

But despite his attitude, Snailman was real. He wasn't pretending to like Mick or anything like that. He was merely connecting the dots objectively. Mick could appreciate that authenticity.

He was stuck in federal custody right now anyway, so he was destined for prison. A deal was way more than he could expect. Maybe this was God giving him some undeserved mercy.

Maybe he could consider this.

It could give me and Donny a way out. If Donny wanted it. He hadn't wanted an escape when Mick had gone rogue in the first place, had insisted he could do more good from the inside. But from the deadly situation faced by supervillain publicists, he wasn't doing nearly enough good.

After a moment, Mick stared at Snailman.

"You must be desperate to bring me on."

"Special Agent Garvey is willing to offer certain incentives."

"Right." He raised his eyebrows. "Private companies paying better for contract heroes?"

He had no reason to look up the information, but in the current feeding frenzy after the Emergence, it would make a lot of sense. Everyone wanted their piece of the pie before federal government regulations passed through Congress. Now the government was trying to catch up.

The hero glowered at him, which was pretty impressive with those eye stalks.

Mick grinned. "They do pay better, don't they?"

"That is not your concern."

"It does if I'm considering working for you." He steepled his fingers over his face. It was probably safe to ask about Cass now. He had his emotions in check. "Where is Cass?"

"Cassandra Robinson is with Special Agent Garvey. She is unharmed and being questioned about her actions in association with you. You might be able to see her soon."

"Might?" Mick tried another bite of protein bar.

"After you're fitted with a neuralepser to deal with your troublesome powers."

The food turned to ash in his mouth.

"A what?"

Chapter Sixteen

Cassie stalked back across the hotel room for the tenth time. Or twentieth. She hadn't been keeping track.

Were the walls closing in? With that hideous yellow wallpaper from the seventies, it felt like it. No one needed that kind of eyesore in their life. Were her captors trying to break her with bad interior decorating?

"They'll have to work harder than that." She pivoted and marched over to the double bed, flopped backward onto the center of the floral coverlet, then winced. Not her smartest idea. The mattress was far from chiropractor approved.

Even then, normally she'd be able to sleep. Cassie could always sleep. But right now, she was wide awake, and she had no idea why. Maybe due to the strange outburst of powers? What had she done, anyway?

She turned her mind from another cycle of useless pondering to study the room. Again. It wasn't much, just the bed, a small metal nightstand with rusty corners, and a lamp. Well, there was also the tiny bathroom with a shower full of questionable stains, one broken light and one working light, and a toilet that wouldn't stop running.

Cassie exhaled a thin stream of air, then called out, "I thought the government had better facilities than this!"

Was it a dumb move? Probably, but her life was threatened daily by supervillains. Compared to that, special agents were small potatoes.

Tension knotted her stomach. At least, Cassie hoped the agents would be small potatoes. Ever since she had woken up on this bed, she hadn't seen Special Agent Garvey. There was no clock in the room, and the curtains were fastened tightly over the windows. She'd tried to peel them back to no avail. It could have been twenty minutes or two hours. And she had no idea what happened to Mick, except that it probably involved a lot of prison time.

Her chest tightened. Yes, he had a record of lawbreaking, but he was Mick. He was trying to be different. He had helped her when he didn't have to, again and again.

They'd been *that close* to kissing. Even if it wasn't a good idea. Or was it? She played with the spine pendant around her neck, remembering his identical tattoo on his chest. He'd played it off as a random mark, but that was bullcrap. It had to be.

But what did that connection even mean? That they'd both gotten hung up on some childhood crush, or was it more than that?

I should have just kissed him. At least she would have had a good memory to go along with the overthinking.

"Augh." She rolled over onto her stomach. It was one thing to choose to live in a tiny campervan, and another thing entirely to be trapped in a dingy hotel room with too much time to think, protein bars that tasted like cardboard, and absolutely nothing to do.

Her fingers traced patterns in the blanket. Who was Special Agent Garvey anyway? She looked just like Anda, but that couldn't be right. Her sister Andromeda was overseas in Bangladesh with Doctors Without Borders. She would never join a government agency.

Then again, from Katrina's strange behavior, it was clear that Cassie's family had been keeping secrets from her. Maybe Anda had a different line of work. Or maybe she wasn't Anda at all, but a genner with a shapeshifting, mind-manipulating, hallucination, or illusion ability.

She shuddered. Those were the worst. Thankfully, that type rarely needed marketing help because they would just use their skills to alter their reputation.

The sound of a door opening jolted Cassie to a sitting position. There stood Anda—Special Agent Andrea Garvey, calm and collected in a navy blouse, slacks, and plain black shoes. Her black hair fell in long, shining sheets on either side of her narrow face, and her brown eyes were unreadable. Cassie scuffed a hand through her own messy ponytail and steeled herself.

The woman definitely looked like her little sister, right down to the high cheekbones and thin lips.

But that didn't mean anything.

The fluorescent light above her flickered, as if the environment needed one more addition to the creepy hotel atmosphere. More nervous energy filled Cassie. She shivered. Somehow, she *knew* the energy had come from the light.

"I'm sorry about the tasing and the sedation. I had to ensure you weren't a threat." The smooth, mellow voice was also perfect Anda. She stepped over to the edge of the bed, her expression wary and concerned.

"Where's Mick?"

"The criminal Michael Bruno, also known as Mick Brown, is safely incarcerated at this moment."

Cassie's shoulders slumped a little. Great, she had gotten him in trouble. Although it had been his idea to start with. But it had freed her from a really bad situation.

I wish he was here.

"It's been a while, Cassie," the agent continued. "I haven't heard from you in months."

Cassie swallowed. "Years, Anda. It's been years since we spoke. The fact that you don't know that suggests you aren't who you pretend to be."

"Or you could be the imposter." Her lips tilted in a tiny smile. "Not that you are. We examined you, tested your blood and your DNA. I know that you're my sister."

"Except that I know my sister wouldn't betray a core family rule to work for the government."

The special agent sighed. "I'm doing what I have to. At least I didn't drop out of law school to work for the enemy."

"I was tricked!" Cassie huffed. "If you aren't Anda, you're doing a great job imitating her 'perfect daughter' attitude. You even have the judgey yoga vibe down pat."

"It wasn't my fault that I—"

"That you what?"

"That I could be quiet and learn and didn't sneak out past curfew to attend prom with a boyfriend I wasn't supposed to have!" She rolled her eyes and pinched the bridge of her nose, sitting on the edge of the bed. "How do you make me do that?"

"Do what?"

"Lose control. I'm an educated professional in leadership, and you just ... just ..."

"Control is overrated. At least, for you. You always had too much of it." Despite her suspicion, Cassie grinned a little. She knew she should be more suspicious, but all of this—it just felt like classic Anda, right down to the fluster. "But about prom, no one saw me. I made sure of that."

She'd even bought a prom dress at a local thrift store. Being homeschooled didn't mean she had to miss out on all the fun, no matter what her parents said. They'd been frustrated that she'd been struggling in her online college classes. In their eyes, more studying was definitely the answer, or maybe some wholesome solo hiking. They didn't have to know her hiking had led to a limo packed with her friends from the after-school art club her parents allowed as an acceptable enrichment activity.

Anda chuckled quietly. "Who do you think covered for you? You were clever, but you were also out too late."

"That was you?"

Her sister nodded with a shy twitch of her lips. "I knew your brain was tired from studying and your energy levels were low.

Walking wouldn't help. You had to be going somewhere else. So I followed you and I saw the limo."

"Hey, thanks." Cassie scooted closer so there was only a foot of space between them. Part of her warmed a little. It was her sister, Andromeda Liwanag Beam. No one else could have known about that. Soon that little sister was getting a bear hug. "Still using all that loopy 'energy' talk, huh? What does that mean?"

Her sister paused. "Our family ... there's no easy way to say this."

"At least you'll be talking more than Katrina."

"Good to know those subroutines are still active. I'll need to deactivate them now that you know—well, if I can parse Mom's coding. It isn't my specialty. Anyway," she exhaled slowly, "we're all genners. I can perceive and manipulate bioelectric energy. It's how I've been able to read people, to a certain extent. I can perceive how their nervous system, their heartbeat, and other systems work and then manipulate that energy. It was a reason I needed to go into medicine. It was a good cover for my abilities. People just assumed I had excellent analytic skills and intuition."

"Wait ... you ... all of you? And no one told me?" A numbness settled over her. Sure, she had suspected a bit last night, especially with Katrina, but hearing it confirmed was another thing entirely.

Mick had been right. They were hiding something.

Anda shook her head. "I didn't want to keep the secret, but they said it was the only way to protect us and you."

"Right. I'm the big mouth who can't be trusted." She moved off the bed and folded her arms across her chest. "Because like always, all of you with your Mensa IQs know way better than me. Why even keep me in the family at all if I'm such a liability?"

Her stomach twisted, and the world seemed to spin around her. How could they?

Her sister stood and held out her hands. "They said they didn't want you to have the burden. You didn't have to hide from anyone. You could have a normal life without anyone tracking you."

"So, what, are the rest of you criminals?" Cassie moved back against the side table, almost knocking over the lamp. It flickered on and off. "I almost wish you were a shapeshifter or some other fake instead of my sister."

Anda blanched. "I'm sorry. I really am. Once I got established on my own, I was going to tell you the truth, but I couldn't find you and—Cassie, be careful!"

"Of what?" The lamp flickered again and died. Sudden energy surged through Cassie. Nothing like what had happened when she had faced down the genners at the checkpoint, but enough to give her a boost. "Am I being too loud again?"

The light above them started blinking in and out.

"You're allowed to be upset. This is hard news."

"Thanks for your permission."

The light went dead. Another small jolt of energy filled her. Cassie felt like she could run a marathon. Although she never had, so maybe she wouldn't make it three miles.

"Do you sprint marathons?"

"Not usually," Anda replied. "We didn't realize that you were a genner too. None of our scanners or tests detected it. I think it's because of what you're doing now, and what you did with the taser earlier. The rest of our family manipulates existing energy, but you can absorb energy from your surroundings to use for yourself. It must have blocked the detection devices."

Cassie's heart pounded in her ears. "That makes sense. But why the powers now?"

"Sometimes genners are late bloomers. But I don't think that's true with you. I have an idea, but I need to consider it more deeply." She sucked in a breath, her gentle voice ragged at the edges. "Cassie, calm down and get control."

"How am I supposed to do that?" The last remaining light fixture fizzled out, and the energy funneled into her body. More energy than she expected. Something from the electrical line? Her veins throbbed with the sudden power that pressed against her skin. "Anda—I'm sorry, I can't figure this out—"

"Cassie!"

Light and electricity blasted out from her in a quick, fierce wave. Her eyes pinched shut, then snapped open. The room was dark. "Anda? Are you okay?"

"I'm fine." A tiny flashlight lit up the room. As soon as Cassie's eyes adjusted, she could see her sister held the light. She was kneeling on the ground, her hair frizzy and clothes singed at the edges but still intact. Her movements were fluid as she rose to her feet. "Your abilities can't hurt me. It's a benefit of sharing the same genetics."

Cassie's shoulders slumped and exhaustion filled her. "Good. I'm sorry about that."

"No need to apologize." Her expression was rueful. "You

haven't been trained, after all. We'll need to work on that. It was a reason you were in this room, away from the main base. But I think we can go there now."

"Why now?"

Anda gave her a searching look. "Your energy reserves seem to be back to their normal, subpar level. I'll need to do additional testing, but it appears your abilities are oddly intertwined with some kind of chronic illness in your body."

"My powers are making me worse?"

"No, it doesn't appear so. It might be the opposite, in fact."

"Good." Cassie yawned. "I thought I was like Mick ..." She paused. "I want to see Mick. Before we go any further."

Anda frowned. "There are other priorities. Including sharing with you the real threat that Power-Up Publicity poses to our family."

Irritation filled her, partly at being bossed around and in part because she was in serious need of a Mountain Dew. "Mick is my friend. He's been helping me. I want to see that he's safe, and I want him to be here for this big explanation you're gearing up for."

"Cassie, you know he's a criminal, right?"

"I had no idea." Cassie's tone was as dry as bone.

Anda's expression turned wry. "Yes, that was a dumb question. Still, you do seem to trust him." She eyed Cassie speculatively. "Maybe he has turned over a new leaf."

"He's trying." Sort of. "Also, he hasn't lied to me my entire life. Unlike you." Was it mean? Yes, it was. But it didn't change the facts or her hurt feelings. "I'm sorry. This is a lot, Anda. I want him there. He makes things easier."

His presence grounded her. Even when he asked inconvenient questions or was a teasing jerk. That was him. She liked him.

"If I don't allow him to join us?"

"You can just knock me out again with a taser or whatever else. I won't talk to you or go with you."

Anda drilled her with a stare. Cassie had no problem ignoring it. Instead, she looked down and fingered the spine pendant that dangled from her necklace.

"Very well." She looked up in time to see Anda nodding slowly. "I will arrange for us to meet in a secure conference room in this facility."

"I want to sit next to him. Also, where are we?"

"He will be cuffed and present in the same room." Her mellow voice took on an edge. "I have invested a lot of time gaining a position of trust and authority in this department. This entire situation must be handled carefully."

Cassie raised her eyebrows. "What department is that?"

Even as she asked, her brain supplied the answer from a news brief she'd read recently. But Anda was already talking.

"Genetically Empowered Nationals Department of the United States—or Gendep for short."

Cassie gave a short laugh. It still sounded ridiculous.

"You're missing a few letters in that abbreviation. Even barely-above-average people like me can tell that. It should be Gendepus."

Anda rolled her eyes. "Come, there's no time to waste.

Power-Up Publicity is already planning their next move. We need to be ready."

Chapter Seventeen

The bag over his head smelled like garlic and bleach. The first Mick remembered from his mother's kitchen. The second just made him want to sneeze. His nose twitched, and he clenched his teeth. No way was that happening.

Instead, he used his other senses as he was pushed through an unknown area. Probably a hallway from the way voices dimly echoed around him. A bit warmer than the cell. His muscles tensed, itching to speed. But between his hands cuffed in front of him with more of that disgusting slime that dried hard as concrete and the bag blocking his vision, Mick didn't have a chance of escaping. This was why he always kept running before he got caught.

I'm going to see Cass. It was one of the few things Snailman had said besides, "Hmmm, it appears the neuralepser isn't working sufficiently," and "Stand in the middle of the room and put the bag over your head." Then the teleporter genner had brought him out with a feeling like walking through a scratchy deep freeze. Odd side effect.

"Stop," Snailman said.

Someone behind Mick jerked him to a halt. The bag was yanked off his head, and he was face to face with a woman with high cheekbones and long black hair. Special Agent Garvey. Sudden anger ripped through him.

"You hurt Cass," he ground out.

"She is fine." Her low voice was equally cutting. "But if you have harmed her in any way, I swear—"

"Swear what? You must have already had someone scan my mind. Or maybe you have a genner who can force me to tell the truth." He raised an eyebrow. "Or do gangs have better genners than the government?"

Garvey scowled at him. "You have been assessed, as has she."

"Then why are you making threats?"

Her eyes narrowed. For a brief moment, Mick felt lightheaded, as though the connections in his brain had slowed. "Just be careful, *Mikey*. I'm willing to give you a chance, but I won't give a second one."

The lightheadedness disappeared. Right, so she had some kind of power that affected physical bodies. Good to know.

Wait. She'd called him Mikey.

"Who are you?"

She ignored the question. "I'm also curious about why the neuralepser didn't work properly."

"It slowed me down enough." When the device had been attached, the medical attendants had made him run on a treadmill. Barely twenty miles per hour. Which made the bag over his head and the slime cuffs even more overkill.

"Your abilities should have been stifled completely." She walked around him, fingering the small, penny-sized metal piece attached to the place where his neck and spine met. He'd been trying not to think about it too much, since he had agreed to wear the power-nullifying device. "Where did your powers originate?"

"That's a second-date question," he retorted. "And I'm already seeing someone."

Or he would be, if he ever got around to asking out Cass, and if she said yes. Wasn't the highest priority at this exact moment.

"Still as mouthy as she is." Garvey tsked. "Get him to the room."

Before he could reply, Mick was pulled into a small conference room with light brown wood paneling and a rectangular table that ran the length. Three gray metal folding chairs lined the table on either side. Snailman settled into one chair, across from a familiar figure.

Relief filled him. Cassie, still in the same sweats from earlier, her purple hair even more tousled and frizzy, and her brown eyes bright.

"Mick!" She grinned and leaped to her feet.

Anda spoke. "Not so fast, Cassie—"

But she was already climbing over the table. His lips curved. It was good to see her acting with her usual spunk. A moment later, she had flung her arms around him. "You're alive."

"Thanks, I had no idea." Warmth filled him, even as he inwardly cursed the concrete slime around his wrists. All he wanted to do was return the hug. After years of being treated as a villain, it felt nice to have someone genuinely happy to see him. "You survived as well."

Over Cassie's head, Garvey scrubbed a hand lightly over her face. "I told you he was safe."

Cassie pulled away enough to study the special agent. "I'm sorry, Anda, but your words aren't as trustworthy as they were before."

Anda? She had used that name earlier. Why did it sound familiar?

The pieces snapped together in his mind. Anda had been the name of Cassie's younger sister. Three years younger, if he remembered correctly.

"You became a federal agent?" he asked. "Isn't that against all the prepper rules?"

"I'm aware of the contradiction with my upbringing."

"So what is your real name?" He glanced between her and Cassie.

Garvey tilted her head at her sister. "You didn't tell him?"

"No. We aren't supposed to. Although I guess there are more reasons for secrecy than what I was told?"

"Your guess is accurate." Garvey pinched the bridge of her nose. "If you would both have a seat, I can begin."

Mick managed to sit down, and Cass sat next to him. Snailman moved to sit across from Cass once more.

"Where'd the rest of your goons go?" Mick asked.

"This is a classified presentation. Only those in this room are permitted to know—well, Wallace already knows." She glanced at Snailman, then eyed Mick. "You are not technically permitted, Mr. Bruno, but it was the only way my sister would cooperate. Considering your potential, it was an acceptable risk."

Cassie smiled sweetly. "Thank you, Anda."

"You're welcome." She gave her sister an aggrieved look, though her eyes softened with affection. Then her gaze moved to Mick, and her eyes narrowed. "I will admit that injury to civilian bystanders is not part of your record."

"I do have some standards."

"Yes, you do. We'll see if they are enough."

Mick repressed a sigh. He didn't care what government stooges thought. But this was getting old. It was another reason he avoided the do-gooder crowd.

Snailman's words echoed back to him, about how Mick could hardly blame people for treating him like a villain if he always acted like one and didn't bother to indicate otherwise. Then there was the offer of inclusion on this government superhero crew. Besides that, Anda was Cassie's sister, and that still seemed to mean something to his friend. If he wanted to be more than friends with her, it would be a challenge. *Did* he want that? The question rang hollow in his mind. He already knew the answer.

"Thanks, Anda." The words came out quiet but true. She could have turned him over to the cops as soon as the feds grabbed him. She could have left him in that cement cell.

Anda nodded. Then she turned to the wall and clicked a tiny object in her palm. In response, the wall parted in two, revealing a large smart monitor.

"Cassie, you might have wondered if Power-Up Publicity had another reason for keeping you in their supervillain publicity division."

"It seemed too convenient," Cassie replied. "And they tricked me into signing up. When I tried to stay in my own apartment, all the utilities failed. I had to move into the company apartment option." She tapped her fingernails against the table. "Then I thought I was being paranoid like Mom and Dad were."

"It isn't paranoia if everyone is actually out to get you." Anda's lips twitched. "Still, I believe we should get on the same page. It will make sharing this easier."

She inclined her head to her sister.

"Finally." Cass turned to him. "I'm Cassandra Liwanag Beam. My sister is Andromeda Liwanag Beam. Liwanag from our mother Aurora Liwanag. Dad's name is Joel Beam."

Something about those names seemed familiar. Like Mick had heard them in passing. But how, if they had been kept secret?

Anda continued. "The reason we kept our lineage private is that we come from two lines of natural genners. And because our family has a history with the CEO of Power-Up Publicity."

Mick narrowed his eyes. "Your family knows Max Fields?"

There was no way. Life couldn't be that weirdly connected.

"When my parents knew him, he was known as Mitty Feldmann. They met at MIT." A picture of Cass's parents next to the CEO flashed up on the screen. All of them looked college aged, arms slung over each other's shoulders. A fourth man with brown skin and a kind smile stood with them, maybe a decade older.

Hell. That just made things more awkward. Although it could be worse. Mick could have had an actual friendship with Max.

Cassie said, "That older man ... have I seen him before?"

"That is Herbert Aldini. He disappeared years ago."

Mick studied the man's face. "He looks kind of like the receptionist who checked me in and out of Power-Up Publicity. Asked me if I knew how to behave, like I was taking his daughter out on a date."

"But could that just be coincidence? Angus is generally friendly and chivalrous." Cassie chewed her lip.

"Hmmm, maybe."

"Herbert disappeared shortly after the events *I was about to relay*." Anda's gentle voice hardened over the last few words. Mick held up his cuffed hands in a "no offense" gesture, his mind still working away at the Max Fields issue. Which might not be an issue, except for Donny. Donny always made things complicated. The kid was lucky he was cute.

She went on. "Mom and Dad aren't that open about the past, even with me. Some of this information I had to find out on my own. But from what I gathered, our parents, Herbert, and Mitty were all friends and worked together. Mitty and Herbert knew our parents were genners. As I mentioned previously, our abilities are hereditary, which makes them stable and powerful. Both family lines have energy powers. Like attracts like."

"So that's real?" Mick had heard the rumor that genners tended to connect with other genners instinctively, especially of the same power type.

"It can be." Anda bit her lip. "Not always, though."

Cassie leaned forward. "How would you know?"

"Moving on, the point is that our parents met in college, fell in love, and became friends with Mitty and Herbert. At the time, the group was interested in how to adapt Mom's solar abilities and Dad's electrical abilities for new ideas in technology. They wanted others to be able to benefit from the off-the-grid lifestyle, and they also thought it would be helpful in developing countries." Anda's face darkened. "But Mitty had another agenda. Our parents discovered that he was doing secret experiments with their blood samples, trying to figure out serums to duplicate their powers in others, only at a highly amplified level. He was jealous of them."

Mick recalled Max's eager face as he surveyed the reports about the results of the serum he'd given Mick. Jealousy sounded about right. Especially with the two years of lockdown afterward, trying to figure out how to recreate the results, among other things.

"That's gross." Cass's face scrunched up. "I'm guessing this didn't end well."

"Doesn't surprise me at all," Mick muttered.

"The other three confronted him, and he said he was only thinking of the greater good. That technology based on their powers would take too long to develop. It was easier and faster to simply make more genners *like* them. Then Herbert revealed that he had hacked Mitty's computer." Anda sucked in a breath. "He had schematics for a number of weapons, genner super-soldiers, and even for an underground system of entrapped genners used to power technology."

Anger rose within Mick. "Your parents destroyed all of his plans, obviously."

"They did. Then they and the rest of our relatives went deep off the grid."

"Then they had me. The broken one." Bitterness laced Cassie's tone.

Compassion gentled her sister's features. "They never meant to imply that."

"Really?" Cassie shook her head. "Where are they, anyway?"

"Your guess is as good as mine." She shrugged.

"That's ... great. I'm just ... I had no idea, Anda! I was stuck in that corporation, almost dying every other day, and if they had just *told* me—"

"I know." Anda sighed.

Mick tugged at the slime restraints. They didn't budge. There was no way he could offer Cass any kind of comfort. He moved closer to her until their shoulders touched. It was lame, but better than nothing.

Should he tell her the truth about his connection to Max Fields? Maybe. Or maybe it would put Donny in the crosshairs and get Mick thrown into a maximum-security prison. Even if he turned CI, would that be enough?

"At least with your powers being subtle, they likely have no idea what you're capable of. If they had, Max would have locked you up."

"Why didn't he?" Her head rested lightly against the side of Mick's shoulder. "They took blood from me at the start. If Max had any samples left of our parents' DNA, they'd know who I really was."

Anda clasped her hands in front of her. "I have no idea—"

Fast, hard knocking at the door interrupted her. Anda stood and turned toward the doorway. "Enter."

A suited agent ran into the room, his face tight. "Agent Garvey, there's something you need to see."

"What is it?"

"On the TV, ma'am."

Anda put her hands on her hips. "Mr. Higgins, please clarify."

The man swallowed. "Power-Up Publicity issued a public statement addressing the kidnapping of one of their employees by a dangerous supervillain and are offering a reward of one million dollars for her immediate recovery and return."

Chapter Eighteen

I knew it. They've been too quiet. Distantly, Cassie was aware of Anda giving orders to the agent, directing the feed to their video screen.

Meanwhile, inside her stomach, knot twisted upon knot. What would they use this conference for? They'd already played an ambitious hand with making a public accusation. A mostly true accusation with just the bald facts. Mostly true accusations were the most dangerous.

"Here we are," Anda announced, turning up the volume. "The public statement."

"About time." Cassie massaged her temples. "They need to get their message out and control the narrative."

Next to her, Mick snorted. "Max Fields would have it no other way."

Something in his tone of voice prodded her. He sounded ... knowing. Cassie glanced at him. "Previous experience?"

He shrugged. Another knot joined the party in her stomach. If he'd been the old Mick from middle school, she'd know he was hiding something by the way he briefly studied his knuckles. But was that true now?

Voices interrupted her train of thought. She turned back to the screen. Two figures stood on the front steps of Power-Up Publicity headquarters in the DC metro area. One was a trim man in his early fifties with a head of well-groomed silver hair, a nondescript square face, and the general demeanor of a no-nonsense businessman, right down to his tailored pinstripe suit.

Cassie tensed. Max Fields looked every inch the self-made corporate king. Even she had to admit that. His image was impeccable. He even had distinguished wrinkles on his pale skin and a long coat draped over his form to appear more regal. The fact that he'd once come after her parents made every polished word and brisk action suspect.

Next to him stood a younger man, barely early twenties, with short auburn hair swept over his forehead, freckles on his tanned skin, and brown eyes that seemed to twinkle at the gathered press even while his expression was serious. He wore a gray suit that likely cost more than Cassie's entire wardrobe.

Next to her, Mick tensed. "Great. Max brought along the pretty boy. As usual."

His eyes drilled into the screen, an intense emotion flickering across his face. Anger? Fear? Something else?

"Who?" Snailman's eyestalks swiveled.

"It's Gavyn Fields." Cass shook her head. "Max's son. He does a lot of PR for his dad. He'll also flirt with anyone he can."

Anda paused the screen, eyeing her. "Anyone? Did you have contact with him?"

"He made the rounds with the junior representatives about

a month ago. The usual corporate platitudes and schmoozing." She rubbed the back of her hand. "Especially with the women, including me."

It hadn't been terrible. He didn't give off a creepy vibe, more like a clueless kid fresh out of college.

Her sister's face sobered. "So they definitely know who you really are."

"Yeah, it's likely. Although, they made a mistake."

"How so?" Snailman glanced her way.

She pursed her lips. "If they were really interested in me as a potential carrier of hereditary abilities, they should have welcomed me in as a superhero publicist. I would have had questions, they could have carefully checked and realized I didn't know the truth, and then they could have sold me a story about how my family didn't care enough to tell me my true lineage." Cass gave a thin smile. "Then they could have welcomed me in and helped me realize my full potential, playing into my need for family and my feelings of betrayal."

Mick gave a low whistle. "Good theoretical manipulation there."

"Working with supervillains does that to you."

"Apparently so. I'm glad we got to you first." Clearing her throat, Anda shifted back to the screen. "Well, let's hear the damage."

Max Fields's message was pretty much what Agent Higgins had said, but played up with professional concern and a side remark about how upsetting it was that an innocent, ordinary woman who simply wanted to do her job was preyed upon by an insidious, unknown villain.

"You mean *you*," Mick muttered, almost growling.

"Why does he say 'unknown?' You saw us." Cassie glanced at Snailman.

"I didn't give Mick's description to the police. I only informed them that I was tracking a supervillain." He slapped his webbed hands together. "In Gendep, we only inform the local authorities if we must, precisely because information could get back to corporations like Power-Up Publicity. It's a perk of being an official government department, albeit a very new one."

Cassie played with her pendant. "But they must have guessed it was Mick. They have cameras everywhere in that place. What game are they playing?"

She turned to Mick. He hadn't reacted to anything she'd said, not even with a sarcastic remark. Instead, he seemed sober. Watchful.

"Not concerned, Mick?"

"Cameras didn't catch anything," he replied shortly.

"Yes, but why not?"

"Back to the press conference," Anda interjected.

Then came a question from a reporter. "Gavyn Fields, did you have any personal connection with Ms. Robinson?"

His expression softened and he leaned forward. "I strive to make direct contact with each branch of Power-Up Publicity at least once a year. We might be a growing corporation, but we still have a heart to see even the newest hire succeed. Ms. Robinson was present during one of my in-person visits. Though we had only a moment, her competence made an impression. She seemed to be a remarkable, resilient woman." He paused and took a quick breath. "It is despicable that anything happened to her. I promise you, I am willing to do whatever it takes to ensure she is safe."

Next to him, Max nodded. "Yes, we will ensure she is safely recovered from this heinous kidnapping."

More questions peppered him from the gathered reporters. Max only waved them off and ascended the stairs into headquarters, his long coat swooping behind him like he was some kind of hero instead the reigning monarch of a company with scummy plans for genners. Gavyn trailed behind him with another winsome smile.

"'Remarkable, *resilient* woman.'" Cassie squinted at the screen. "What a strange word to use. We barely spoke. How would he know I'm competent?" She rubbed the back of her hand again at a particular scar.

Anda raised an eyebrow. "Where did you speak?"

She shuddered, leaning a bit closer to Mick. "I was in an alcove, trying to get up the nerve to walk to my office. A metal manipulator had tried to strangle me with my own stapler the day before."

"And then?" Anda pressed.

"I see where you're going, and ... you're not wrong. I probably did look like a wreck, so he was trying to encourage me. Although I didn't tell him the details of my job. The confidentiality agreement included not sharing the behavior of clients with anyone." Cassie frowned, trying to recall the rest of the meeting. "He told me I was right to be scared, and that it was healthy. But if I made it a few more months, I would have amazing things ahead of me. Then he kissed the back of my hand."

"He was flirting with you?"

An image of Gavyn Fields flashed in her mind. Those sincere puppy-dog eyes. The earnest way he assured her things would get better. It was like he could feel her anxiety.

"No, I don't think so. I mean, he was being him. As I said, he flirts with a lot of people, but he seemed genuinely concerned."

Snailman blustered. "A likely tactic to win your trust while vulnerable."

"Seriously?" Cassie glared at him. "I'm not that gullible."

"Of course you aren't, but even so, we have to consider all angles here," Anda said. "He was playing the press, implying there was some connection between you and him. It makes him seem relatable and human. A smart PR move."

"He wanted people to think that, sure, but he only said that it was despicable that anything happened to me and that he wanted me safe." They were interesting word choices. "We're missing something here. I know a supervillain in my gut, Anda. He ... something's off."

Her sister studied her thoughtfully. "Interesting observation. Don't you think, Mick?"

His head snapped up, his face a mask. "If you say so."

"I do. Also, do you know that my clearances and status give me access to a number of public and private databases?"

"You mean you have access to hackers." His lips curled. "Good for you."

By now, Cassie's stomach had been replaced by one giant knot. What was going on here? "Are you accusing him of something, Anda?"

Her sister shook her head. "Not at all. I'm simply making him aware of information. Such as those computer experts who are also quite skilled at recovering data from cell phones. Even cell phones with an impressive self-incineration process."

Mick could have been carved from stone. "That sucks."

Cassie rested a hand on his arm. "Why? Mick, can you clue me in here?"

"If I do, it could be dangerous."

"For who?"

His jaw worked, and he refused to meet her eyes. "For my brother."

"His half-brother," Anda put in, her voice soothing but flat. "A paternal connection."

Paternal. Pater. "So you're related on your father's side? Okay, sure." Cassie fiddled with the end of her ponytail. It felt like the knowledge was right in front of her. Augh, it was not fair to ask her brain to do puzzles after the events of the last few days. "How is that a problem?"

Mick turned to face her, the mask dropping away for a moment. His brown eyes softened, with a shade of pleading in them. Something about the gaze seemed familiar. Like someone else's she had seen so recently on the screen.

Years ago, her friend had mentioned he was adopted in an

off-hand way. It never seemed to matter much to him, so Cassie hadn't pressed.

Suddenly, it mattered a lot more now.

"Oh." The knots loosened and sank into the pit of her stomach. She squeezed his arm. "You're his ..."

"Yeah," he breathed. "Unfortunately. I'm Max Fields's other son."

Chapter Nineteen

Cass stared at him, eyes wide, her face inches from his as she leaned in. What was she searching for? Hoping for?

If she was afraid of him, she wasn't showing it. There was no hatred on her face either. Only intent curiosity and something warmer.

Dang, how could she be so ... her? Didn't she get that he was related to bad guys?

"What, do I have something in my teeth?" He pitched his words low. The last thing he wanted was Anda butting in.

"I can't tell, beanpole. You don't smile." She gave him a light shove, backing away slightly. Then she patted his arm again. "I trust you."

He raised his eyebrows. "It's that easy, huh?"

It couldn't be. Not after all she'd been through.

"I mean, I'd like to know more, obviously. But all this time, you've been against Power-Up Publicity, so I'm guessing you're not a fan of your ... biological dad?" He nodded in response to her tonal question, and she continued. "So there's that. Plus, you're in handcuffs and all, so even if I was worried about a physical threat, which I'm not, you aren't one. Also, trusting someone isn't easy.

It's a choice to believe in them and give them that grace. Trust takes guts. And you've heard my family's dirty laundry at this point, so here we are. Yeah."

She exhaled and flopped back in her chair, looking at him expectantly. "What's the rest of the story?"

Mick smiled despite himself. Who even was this woman? A bundle of contradictions, of emotions and smarts and suspicion and openness.

Asking her out had just moved up as a priority.

"A question the rest of us would like answered as well," Snailman said, stylus poised over a tablet computer. "For posterity, of course."

"Right, you want me to talk for your files."

"Not for government records," Anda said. "For our personal records. The saga of our family's history is not a matter of public record, and I would prefer that it stay private. Wallace is in agreement."

Snailman swiped at the screen. "This is noted."

"The slimy boy scout isn't lockstep with the feds?" Mick scoffed.

"My powers are the result of an out-of-control government research project. I'm loyal to my country and the law, but neither are infallible."

"Huh." He could work with that. Maybe.

Donny's words echoed back to him. *It is despicable that anything happened to her. I promise you, I am willing to do whatever it takes to ensure she is safe.*

It all but confirmed that getting Cass out had been the reason Donny had sent him to the St. Louis branch of Power-Up Publicity. Had it been due to her family history? Their connection?

Mick had no way of knowing. All he had was government custody and the agents' assurance that they wouldn't turn on him. Ordinarily, it wouldn't have been enough.

But he'd seen how Donny had kept his hands in his coat pockets throughout the press conference. A way to hide that they were shaking. The way he had had twitched his nose, which he only did when he was wearing makeup to cover up the dark circles and paleness caused by meds. It had been a hard day for him, but their jerk of a father had forced him to do PR anyway. All because Donny was winsome.

"Fine. Two conditions."

Anda tugged at her blazer. "Name them."

"You retrieve or otherwise help Gavyn Adonis Fields escape Power-Up Publicity. He's sick, has been for a while, and he keeps letting Fields experiment on him because it gives him access to help others at Power-Up Publicity." Mick's jaw worked. "It's gone on too long."

The special agent paused, then nodded. "I should be able to pull a few strings and manage that. It won't be immediate, though. These matters take time. We're still working on creating protocols and procedures at Gendep. Max Fields is a known problem with a loud publicity team, but not an imminent threat."

"How can you say that?" Cass exclaimed. "We know he was after us. Genners ambushed us at one of the checkpoints."

Anda cleared her throat. "That wasn't him. Another department in Gendep was sent after you without notifying me."

"What?"

"Government communication is terrible. Albatrosses with chalkboards would be better. I'm sorry." She shifted in her seat. "You mentioned another condition, Mick?"

"I want to be on the team that gets him out. He's my brother."

"I'll help too," Cass added.

Anda glanced between them, her lips quirking. "It sounds like you're volunteering to join forces with the government."

Mick glowered. "I didn't say that."

"We're still working on the logistics of teams, but it will be a requirement to sign on in order to be part of operations."

"... I'll think about it." He already had been, but having it mandated through a government deal felt worse than making the choice himself.

"I hope you do. Do we have those requests, Wallace?"

His eyestalks bobbed. "I have every detail so far." Snailman turned to Mick. "If there are no other conditions, go on."

Mick set his bound hands on the table. "It's not that complicated. Twenty-six years ago, Max Fields knocked up my biological mother in a fling. She gave me up in a closed adoption and is dead now. I knew I was adopted but didn't really care too much either way. Then when I went under for transformation via serum, turns out Fields was quietly funding the illegal powers clinic because he wanted transformation research. He found me."

"And after that?"

He shrugged. "He tried to get me to sign on to the grand and glorious dream. He didn't tell me any details about the Beams, just that he was creating a better world that I should be part of. I didn't care, didn't want in—I'd already had a rough situation with one dad. So instead, he kept me under lock and key in a private house. It was there that I met Donny."

A skinny kid of eleven with too-big eyes behind thick glasses and a fondness for cartoon t-shirts. At first, Mick had been certain that his half-brother was a plant to gain his sympathy. But he'd quickly seen that Donny knew less than him. He was a project to Fields, like everything else.

"We hung out and became friends. I got my GED under extreme duress of enforced tutors, and then at age eighteen, I managed to escape with Donny's help. I haven't had contact with Fields since."

"So after that, you ended up in gangs?" Cass asked.

"I couldn't be anywhere Fields would find me. Criminal life fit the bill. Until it didn't, and I started trying to help the good guys or at least ensure the baddies wouldn't succeed. All through, I kept in touch with Donny. He'd tip me off about opportunities to screw over Power-Up Publicity. When I stopped by the St. Louis branch, I thought it was another chance to do some damage. Then I came across Cass." His lips tilted up in a small smile. "I guess it actually worked out better to hurt Fields than I could have hoped for."

She rolled her eyes. "Gee, thanks. Glad to know I'm ammunition in your family feud."

"Yeah, it was convenient." He grinned at her.

"See if I ever kiss you—I mean, I'm going to sic Katrina on you." She pressed her lips together. "Um, so that's it. What's next?"

"Apparently not kissing," Snailman deadpanned. He turned to Anda. "I'll need to do follow-up research, but his answers provide satisfactory data."

"Good." Her eyes fixed on Mick, seemingly less amused than her slimy colleague. "I agree. The preliminary data from our truth assessment is promising. Still, you'll be returned to your cell for the present."

Anda stood, giving a tiny wave to indicate the others should do likewise. Snailman joined her immediately. Well, he could do that. They weren't headed back to a cinderblock cell. Mick rolled his neck back and forth, then rolled his shoulders. If his fingers hadn't been trapped in a slime prison, he would have cracked his knuckles.

"Any time, you two." The special agent rolled her eyes.

Next to Mick, Cassie hadn't moved. "Where am I going? Back to that hideous hotel room? Because I would rather camp out here than there."

Anda's expression softened. "No, you will be given a room in our regular facilities."

"One that has a working toilet and food that isn't protein bars made from wood shavings?"

"You treated your own sister like that? Shame." Mick leaned back in his chair, affecting nonchalance while real irritation filled him. Cass seemed to have enough physical crap to deal with as it was. Couldn't Anda and the stupid feds respond better? "You're not making signing up look very good. My villain dad offered me a swanky office with an executive assistant, a Mercedes, and a salary."

"Consider that your other option is prison," Anda snapped. She rubbed her forehead.

Cass stood up at that, nudging Mick to do likewise. Her peeved attitude had flipped abruptly to regret. "All right, I'll go with you for now. It's just a lot to take in."

"I know. As I said, I wish this had all gone differently." A glimmer of humor returned to her eyes. "You need to rest, Cassie. After all, your training begins tomorrow."

"My training?"

"No power suppressor like you shoved on me? I guess nepotism does count for something."

Cassie made a sound of protest. "Really, Anda? You did that to him?"

"Yes. He's a criminal." She tugged at her coat. "You're my sister, and things are complicated. I'll explain tomorrow."

Chapter Twenty

Cassie stared at her reflection in the small mirror over the tiny dresser in her nondescript room. The four scars on the right side of her face stood out in the harsh fluorescent lighting, which also brought out the dark circles under her eyes and those pebbled acne scars.

"This is why makeup was invented," she muttered, yawning. "And Mountain Dew."

Neither of which she had been given yesterday when Anda had dropped her in this room. There had been actual food—government-issue salad, dry chicken cutlets in gravy, and roasted potatoes—on the small table tucked in a corner, as well as three giant bottles of water. In the small adjacent bathroom were cleansing products in plastic dispensers and a small pouch of basic toiletries. In the drawers were government-issue sweatpants and tops, and some variety of plain underclothes. Even the coverlet on the bed was gray.

It's clean. It's what I have.

"Not actually true. I have Katrina." Her campervan with the custom mattress and special pillows was somewhere in a garage in the facility. Along with Mick, still shoved away in a cell. That had to be terrible for a speedster used to running wherever he went. Now he was tethered with the neuralepser and waiting for the verdict from the feds.

How is this any better? I'm locked in this room. Breakfast had been brought a few hours ago by a stone-faced agent.

She stretched her arms over her head and twisted back and forth, trying to loosen the painful tightness in her back. Government-issue mattresses were slabs of concrete.

And she was a lame twenty-six-year-old whose body didn't understand that it was young.

God, help me get through this. Anda seemed to be on Cassie's side. But she also seemed to be on the government's side.

"At least your hair is still purple. Small wins, right?" Cassie told her reflection. She tugged at the sweatshirt, then glanced at the clock on the wall. 10 a.m. "Any second now ..."

Knocking sounded from the door.

"Cassie? Are you ready?" her sister asked.

"Yup!" Finally, it was time to get out of this place. She grabbed the plastic tray with the remains of her breakfast—fruit salad, oatmeal, sausage links, orange juice—and walked over to the door. "When do we start?"

A quick sound of locks clicked and deadbolt sliding, then her sister opening the door. She was also dressed in sweats and sneakers, with an official-looking badge clipped to her waist. Her hair was in a sleek bun.

"You're ready on time." It wasn't exactly a question.

Cassie pulled up a smile. At least she could talk to an actual person. "I did graduate and hold down several jobs, Anda." She held out the tray. "What do I do with this and the other one from supper?"

"Just leave them in the room. Someone will be by later to collect them."

Because this room wasn't hers. There was no guarantee of privacy.

"All right." She put the tray back on the table and returned to the door. "So, where are we going for this training?"

Anda tilted her head. "Outside. Follow me."

She led the way through a few different hallways, all with white walls and flat gray flooring. Everything smelled vaguely like antiseptic. "How did you sleep last night?"

"Not good. The bed wasn't great. But at least the bathroom had a tub." A hot soak had helped a little.

"I try." Anda shook her head. "I'm sorry. With your unexpected arrival, I haven't had time to see to everything. Things were easier before Congress officially created Gendep. There was a lot less paperwork. It's amazing how many regulations a single oversight committee can create in a few days."

The floor began slanting upward toward a door at the far end. Cassie's heart leaped. *Freedom!*

"So before, Gendep was illegal? Or one of those covert government organizations that conspiracy theorists talk about on their blogs or streaming channels?"

"The second." Anda put her hand on an electric scan-pad, then they exited onto a sidewalk bordering a small parking lot. A squat parking garage took up one corner.

"Mom and Dad would be so proud."

She snorted. "Mom and Dad cut off contact as soon as they discovered I worked for the government."

"Yeesh, I'm sorry, sis." She gave Anda a side hug. "Same for when I went to work for an evil corporation."

Anda briefly returned the hug. "I made my choice, and I don't regret it. Genners need to be on the front lines of government departments so that we can define the rules. I've already filed six appeals to some of the new regulations. One has been granted, two are pending, three are waiting review." She began striding across the parking lot to a span of grass about the size of a soccer field on the other side.

Cassie half-jogged to keep up with her sister. "What about Mick?"

"I've been in contact with the General Chamber about his situation. It *is* the government, Cassie. Nothing moves fast. For a situation like his, it will probably take weeks."

"Weeks? Stuck in that cell?" Cassie's heart sank. She managed to catch up to her sister as they reached the middle of the field. "That can't be healthy for him. He's already got the power-dampener on. Why does he have to be in solitary?"

Anda sighed. "He's a supervillain, Cassie. You remember that, right?"

"You heard his story. It's more than that."

"But it isn't less."

"You see that he's different. He's changed! He gave you all this dirt on his villain dad, for crying out loud!"

Her sister's yoga-zen voice turned as stony as her face. "I included that in my report, but there is nothing else I can do."

"Nothing you want to do, you mean. Because to you, he's still just a villain."

"And you're my sister who met him while in an emotionally vulnerable place."

"So you think I have no discernment?" Cassie huffed. "Unbelievable. *Older* sisters are supposed to be overprotective, not younger sisters."

"I had to improvise when my older sister decided she would rather rebel, sneak around, and work for an evil corporation!"

"That wasn't my fault!" Cassie stepped back, suddenly lightheaded. "I don't need this. I already got terrible sleep in a sucky bed, there's no Mountain Dew in this place, my friend who risked his life for me is stuck in a concrete prison, and everything is spinny—"

A hand gently touched her shoulder. "I'm sorry." Her voice held quiet sympathy. "Although Mountain Dew is terrible for you."

She fought through the cloudiness in her mind. "It's the only thing that gives me energy."

"Other things can do that too. That's why we're out here."

Cassie blinked, forcing the surroundings to come into place. "We're outside because ... you don't want me to accidentally drain the base's power grid. With what power? It hasn't shown up since the hotel room."

"That's the problem we need to fix today. You need to learn how to call it up and shut it down. Once you do that, you can have access to more of the facility."

"So I'm also a prisoner right now?"

Anda rubbed the bridge of her nose. "Your room is located in an area that can be isolated from the rest of the power grid."

"I just said that the power hasn't shown up again."

"Which means it's volatile."

"But why lock me in my room? I was given no key card, and I tried the door. Multiple times." Cassie's shoulders tightened at Anda's closed-off expression. Her sister had been cautious earlier in the conference room, but she'd still spoken freely. Why not here? "Both of the times my abilities emerged were under extreme situations. One where Mick's life was in danger and the other where I was trapped in a hideous hotel room while you told me my family had been lying to me for my entire life. Otherwise, my powers just don't show. So why lock me up?"

Instead of answering, Anda pivoted and strode across the field. This time, Cassie didn't try to catch up and merely followed at her slower pace. There was no point in using precious energy, especially because she was already having more body aches. There was ibuprofen in her purse, which she hadn't been given back.

Another sign that she was actually a prisoner.

I could just ask her for pain meds. Cassie rubbed her spine pendant. *But also ... why didn't she give me my purse back?*

Her sister paused at the edge of the field, which was bordered by woods. She knelt briefly, then stood. Her mouth was set in a firm, thin line, her hands at her sides, but her eyes—her eyes were sad.

"You look like you did the day we found that runaway puppy outside the Winn-Dixie." Cassie came to a stop in front of her. "Mom said we had to take it to the shelter, remember?"

"*No ifs, ands, or buts.*" Anda mimicked their mother's tone, glancing around.

Then she threw a rock the size of an apple at Cassie's head.

Cassie yelped and ducked—or tried to. Her back chose that moment to spasm with pain, which meant she froze instead like a deer in headlights.

Thank God her sister had bad aim. The rock only grazed her left cheek before falling to the ground.

She winced, rubbing at the spot while blinking away tears at the fading pain. "What the crap, Anda?"

"I'm sorry." Another rock sailed her way. "Duck, Cassie! You're good at that."

"Not when I've been shoved in a room with an awful bed where I can't even stretch!"

This time she managed to sidestep—only for two other rocks to deflect off her pants. Cassie heaved a breath and grabbed a nearby tree, steadying herself. "What's wrong with you?"

"I had to test my theory. You couldn't be warned. Here." She walked over to Cassie and held out a tiny packet which held a bandage and a disinfectant swab. "It's extraordinary. Your powers reached out only to push away the rocks. I think your body instinctively absorbs the kinetic energy—but not entirely. As if somehow a part of you is aware that you need to appear injured."

Staring at the bandage, Cassie shook her head. "You're kind've messed up, sis. You know that?"

Slowly she grabbed the materials and started treating the scrape. Injuries at Power-Up Publicity had made it easy enough to feel for cuts.

"I didn't have a choice. I had to surprise you. Your powers don't show up on any devices. I can't even detect them with my own abilities."

"You said powers don't work on family."

"Yours are an exception, at least when it comes to evading detection." Anda brushed a wisp of hair back into her ponytail. "That level of subconscious, instinctive control is incredible."

"Does this mean I can stop being a prisoner? Or at least, I can be confined to the base instead of that room?"

"I think so, although it would be a risk."

Cassie shoved the used packet into a pocket. "For everyone on the base?"

"No, for you."

The words jolted her, and she stood up straight. "What do you mean? The government is out to get me? You're not really working for them voluntarily? I knew it—"

"Stop." Anda held up a hand. "I'm not saying any of that. But had I known your powers were this complicated, I might not have brought you in. I'm trying to recruit genners who are simple to quantify. Ones that have easily understood abilities."

"You mean camera-friendly." The words came out wooden.

"Exactly. When our agents mentioned that you had absorbed and deflected energy, I thought it was that straightforward. That

I could do damage control. But your abilities have developed in unique ways that might make the ords uncomfortable. Especially since they can't be tracked or analyzed." She sighed. "Walk with me. There's a comfortable spot nearby."

Cassie raised her eyebrows. "No more rocks?"

"No more rocks. I promise."

She followed her sister into the damp, green forest. Anda paused by clusters of thick moss between tree trunks and sat down. "I like this place. It reminds me of the spot in the Virginia Highlands where we stayed for a year. Plus, there are no cameras or people around."

"Yeah, that was a nice place." Cassie moved gingerly to her knees, then settled onto a plushy bit of moss and leaned against a tree trunk. Her heart still fluttered in her chest uncertainly. "So, my powers?"

"Right. I think your powers actually emerged when you were a lot younger, but they were immediately put to use instinctively."

"Doing what?"

"Compensating for your physical condition. I did some preliminary scans after we ... after you were—"

"Tased and taken to a government facility against my will?"

"Yes, that. You have markers for an autoimmune disorder. Chronic fatigue syndrome is most likely. You had Q fever at age four, so that might have caused some issues. Chronic inflammation is also a possibility."

"I never knew that."

"You know our parents never made a big deal about those things.

It took some time and research to be able to chart our family medical history." Anda shrugged. "But I theorize that your ability to absorb energy stepped in and started drawing small amounts from your surroundings to compensate. Your body did all of this subconsciously to survive. Yet you also didn't take too much, perhaps because of our parents' admonitions to never stand out or draw attention."

Cassie stroked the moss on either side of her. "I did all that without realizing it?"

"It's a theory, but it's the best one I have. The mind-body connection with genners is very new science. And as I said, your powers cannot be studied with current devices. It was probably one reason why Power-Up Publicity never discovered your abilities. You had already grown used to hiding them by then, and you knew you weren't safe."

"Huh." She turned the theory over in her head as she played with a small twig in her fingers. All the near misses or injuries that should have been worse than they were. "But why do I still have the body aches and stiffness?"

Anda shrugged. "I honestly don't know. Maybe you just fell into certain patterns with your abilities. Pain can be familiar on its own. Perhaps now you can compensate more if you draw more energy? This is all new territory."

"Right, you keep mentioning that." She paused, looking up. "I'm not safe here either."

The words were flat and sure. Maybe she couldn't connect the dots mentally as well as Anda, but she could work with what was in front of her. In this light, everything Anda did looked more like keeping Cassie away from something. Or someone.

A regulation-happy government wouldn't be pleased with a weird genner they couldn't figure out.

Anda swallowed. "As I said, if I had known ... but I don't know what other options you have. I can't tell you where Mom and Dad are because they're off the grid. Power-Up Publicity is on a manhunt to find you. I'm out of ideas." The façade cracked for a moment, revealing exhaustion and desperation. "Please, just work with me, all right? I'm not the enemy."

Cassie stared at her sister. Despite herself, threads of compassion filled her from a place deep inside. An answer to unspoken prayers, because she sure as heck was struggling for sympathy in her own strength. She hadn't asked to be grabbed. Maybe she and Mick could have found their own space somewhere.

Then I wouldn't know about my powers or family.

That was helpful. And just because Anda didn't have ideas didn't mean there weren't any. Cassie needed to explore the base a little and get the right handle on things. Power-Up Publicity was still out there spreading lies about her. She wasn't going to hide in a government facility waiting for them to strike.

First, she needed to start trying to use her abilities.

"Okay, let's do this." She stood up, brushing off her pants. "Probably should get back out to the field before anything looks weird, right?"

"Yes, we should." Once they were back in the middle of the grassy expanse, Anda continued. "The first step is you need to intentionally absorb energy."

"How? From where?" Cassie looked around. "There's just grass and trees here. The cars aren't even turned on."

"Plants collect radiant energy. The ground houses geothermal energy. And speaking of radiant energy, the sun is shining." She pulled out her phone and tapped away at the screen. "I'll have some books sent to your room."

"Or you could just send files over a phone." Cassie looked longingly at the device.

Her sister hesitated, then spoke. "You aren't cleared for one yet. I filed the paperwork—"

"For a *phone*? Wow, you have gone white-collar stooge." She winked. Never mind that she'd done the same at Power-Up Publicity.

Anda made a face at her. "I'll see what I can do. Meanwhile, the lesson is simple. Draw energy from your surroundings. Use it. Then stop using it." She scuffed her sneaker along the ground. "The grass is even green. Like Mountain Dew."

"Mountain Dew has more electric yellow in it."

"This is a problem for so many reasons."

"Killjoy. Have you even tried it?"

Her sister scoffed. "I've never had the urge."

"You're missing out." Cassie grinned, then stared at the grass. "Okay, absorb the grass."

"No, absorb the energy *from* the grass. Kneel down and make physical contact with the blades if you need to. Try closing your eyes." Her voice turned low, almost hypnotic. "Sense the energy.

Focus on what it feels like—your perception will be unique to you. Then draw it into yourself."

Well, I might as well get comfortable. Cassie flopped down on the grass, resting her hands the soft blades. She closed her eyes, trying to reach out and feel something. Anything.

A strange sense of something tickly pinged her senses then disappeared, as though shut behind a door.

"I can't."

"What happened?"

"I thought I felt something, and then it was gone."

Anda's tone was measured. "Maybe you'll have to push back. Your abilities have been held close to you your entire life. They won't be used to extension into the world."

"I guess that makes sense." Cassie tried to focus again, pressing into the darkness, trying to find the tickly feeling. There it was, like a silky ribbon flowing through her fingers.

Then out again.

"What were you doing the last time you used your powers?"

"I was protecting Mick from an energy blast and ..." Cassie swallowed. "I was in the hotel room, trying to escape. I felt trapped."

"Hmmm. Protection and escape. What about ... need?"

"Need? Apparently I've been using enough to get by."

"You need to prove that you can do this, and then you'll get key-card access to the cafeteria, which has Mountain Dew."

"Now you're talking!"

Cassie reached out toward the energy ribbon. It was a wily thing, slipping this way and sliding that way, teasing her.

All right then, let's play. Cassie mentally dodged with the energy like it was a kind of dance. Finding the rhythm in the way it flickered at the edge of her perception, then darted away.

Forward and back. Forward and back.

Until it was tangled up in itself. She grabbed it quickly and felt the energy fill her like a shot of lightning.

"Got it!"

"Yes, you did. Open your eyes."

Cassie blinked, the world coming into focus.

"I did it!" She looked down to where her hands touched the grass and yelped. The blades were brown and dead. "I killed them."

She'd taken the life from a healthy, living plant. And it wasn't because she forgot to water it, like the house plants she'd failed for years. Although had she just sucked the energy from them? This put all of her horticultural issues into new light.

"You took the energy out of the grass, yes." Anda eyed her patiently. "Now release it. Put it back into the grass."

She pushed the energy out with a whoosh. The grass started standing up again and turning a fresh, healthy green. Her shoulders slumped.

"Does this mean I have villain powers? Because I kill things?" Cassie frowned. "Maybe it's like food. Like a salad, only without having to actually eat it."

Anda nodded firmly. "Yes, think of it like that. Now you just need to practice that at least twenty-five more times. After that, we'll work on geothermal energy, and then" —she pulled out another phone, this one a cheap flip-phone— "we'll move on to electrical energy and sound energy."

Cassie squared her shoulders. "Okay. Let's do this."

Mountain Dew was waiting for her.

Chapter Twenty-One

Anda was trying. Cassie had to give her sister credit for that. It wasn't enough for the long-term—they both knew that—but it was something.

At least now she had access to the cafeteria, the gym, and the garage that held Katrina. Cassie had taken to sleeping in the campervan at night, only using the gray room when she wanted a hot bath. Her purse and other personal effects had been returned to her, minus the cell phone. Also, Anda had dug up a tablet computer loaded with ebooks and audiobooks, along with a few basic games like Tetris and solitaire. It was better than nothing—apart from the hour of training each morning and two hours of training each afternoon, Cassie had nothing else to do. The agent types around were polite but stiff, focused on their specific assignments.

"From being trapped in Power-Up Publicity to being trapped with the government," she muttered, poking at the tray of half-eaten food in front of her.

And there was no Mick. After four days, she knew that her world needed more Mick in it. Since Anda couldn't fix this problem, among many others, Cassie would simply solve it herself.

Which, at this moment, meant hanging out in this exact spot in the cafeteria. Because this was where Snailman sat every day for dinner, by himself with a book, for thirty minutes starting at 6:45 p.m. and ending at 7:15 p.m. The workers at the food line had assured her of this, after some friendly conversation and using a tiny bit of her powers to cool down a glitchy, overpowered heat lamp. Thermal energy was getting easier to play with, and she didn't mind the extra energy. It had eased some of the pain in her shoulders.

Now, she waited. Cassie rested her forehead against the white plastic-coated tabletop, her fingers playing idly with her paper cup of Mountain Dew.

Mick, I wish you were here. He didn't always talk, but even his quiet presence was soothing. She was barely five foot two. A big guy next to her who wanted to protect her wasn't a bad thing. Especially when he was easy on the eyes and had a tattoo of her pendant on his chest for reasons she was still trying to parse, although the general analysis was positive.

"Are you bored?"

Snailman's nasal, oddly resonant voice broke through her thoughts. She looked up at him. He wore plain blue pants and a gray long-sleeved tunic that seemed to be standard around here besides the business attire. She wore the exact same outfit—it was better to save her everyday clothes for when she got out of here.

"A little bit." She managed a smile. "There isn't really anything for me to do. Even my ride has been taken care of."

That, Cassie was fine with. Let someone else deal with the gray water and black water tanks. She trusted that Anda wouldn't let anyone into Kat's innards where their parents performed their secret genius work.

"Good." His eye stalks swiveled around, studying her from different angles. His rough webbed hands rested on the table, the fingers twitching. "The criminal has asked about you."

Her smile widened. "Did he ask you to tell me that?"

"No. I might be a biological abnormality due to a close call with nuclear snails, but I do have a heart." The hero paused. "He said to tell you that he wasn't dead yet. I'm assuming that was Monty Python. And that you shouldn't go through the fire swamp without him because an R.O.U.S. would definitely take you down."

Monty Python and The Princess Bride. Clearly, she had to marry this man, even if he was a villain and a butt who thought she'd get taken down by a giant rodent. She chuckled. "Good to know he hasn't annoyed you that much."

"No, although he does like to provoke."

Cassie tilted her head. "Come to think of it, I don't know your actual name. Is it Wally?"

Anda had used it once or twice during their previous meeting, but there had been a lot of reveals at that meeting. Way too much to keep track of one name.

Besides, it would be good to get on better footing with him before she shamelessly asked to see Mick.

He paused. "Heroes use code names for our security. The lack of proper laws means that a layer of anonymity is vital."

"Even if you look like a ... snail?"

"Even so. Gendep prefers us to be discreet at this point. No heroes are required to reveal their true identities unless they choose."

"Right. That makes sense."

Snailman's eye stalks swiveled independently right and left. Finally, they turned back to her. "It's Wallace. Wallace Cooper."

Ah yes, that sounded familiar.

"It's nice to meet you, Wallace. Or do you prefer Cooper?"

"Wallace is fine. My cousin Sheldon prefers to be called Cooper."

"I see." Cassic nodded. "Have you been part of Gendep long?"

He took a bite of some kind of beefy sludge on his plate. It was odd to see a greenish human mouth and blobby nose with the snail features, but he seemed kind enough, and that was more important. "Since its inception. I had been working on a government research project studying the impact of nuclear test sites on snails and their slime. A longitudinal study, you understand. It had been decades and decades in the making, and I was honored to continue the work, but ..." He took another bite, chewing thoughtfully. "It didn't end up that way. There was an accident. Then this happened to me."

Wallace gestured to the eye stalks and held out his webbed hands.

"What about the shell on your back?"

"Oh, that holds snacks, my scientific toolkit to gather samples, a comic book. I created it after my transformation. I thought it fit the overall theme."

Cassie laughed. "That's a great idea! It works. I'm sorry, I just assumed—"

"That the transformation had taken over my whole body? A lot of people do, and they make comments, some of them both creative and lewd." He shrugged. "Heroes come from all kinds of places. Nature does what it will." The snailman looked at her. "What about your powers?"

His blunt, direct words reminded her of one of the reasons they were talking. Not just because she missed people and Wallace was surprisingly friendly, but also because she wanted to see Mick.

"They're doing all right, I guess. I've learned enough control not to be an immediate threat to the world around me."

Her tone was dry, but Snailman only looked serious. "An important milestone." He paused. "Ms. Robinson—"

"Cassie is fine."

"Cassie," he amended. "This conversation has been tolerable, but I surmise that by it you are hoping for us to grow familiar so you can see Mick."

She almost choked on her Mountain Dew. "Really? You think that?"

"Your sister warned me that you're 'capable of talking a camel into polar fleece and snow boots.' Astonishing, since camels aren't capable of speech." He fixed her with a searching look. "Have you started that part yet?"

Cassie groaned softly. It figured that Anda would try to ruin her plans. "I *do* like talking to people, Wallace."

"That doesn't answer my question."

When in doubt, just be straightforward. "I mean, sure. I'd like to see Mick. He's my friend, after all. Why wouldn't I try to see him?"

Especially since there was no way she was leaving this base without him.

Snailman pushed away his tray. "Your logic holds, but he isn't allowed visitors at this time."

Her brain latched on to the operative word. "What if I wasn't a visitor?"

"Explain."

"What if I was there for additional training? After all, Mick is skilled in different kinds of combat. It would be useful to practice my abilities in a more active way rather than just simple energy transfers."

The hero folded his arms. "Now it seems like you're endangering a prisoner of the US government."

"Except that I'm not, because we're friends and Mick is powerful. So we won't want to hurt each other. It would just be fun—and productive and valuable—to have a different person to work with my abilities." Cassie gave him her most disarming look. "Besides, Anda mentioned that maybe he would be joining a team. Wouldn't getting practice with others as a potential team be helpful?"

Wallace's eye stalks swiveled in a way that could have been suspicion. "I suppose it would be."

"So, why not?"

"I don't know."

She allowed a bit of pleading to enter her voice. "Just thirty minutes? Please. You did say you had a heart."

He stood up, grabbed his tray, and walked over to the dish room window. Cassie followed him with her cup of soda. Her stomach twisted uneasily. Would this work? Was he blowing her off?

He was probably ignoring her. Too much of a rule follower. Her shoulders slumped. Ah well, it'd been worth a try.

"Thirty minutes. Tail me to the prison area, and I'll get you inside the room."

"Really?"

"You heard nothing." Snailman paused. "But follow me. Hopefully Paula will like you, or at least be preoccupied with her book. Otherwise, this will be harder."

He led her through several hallways to an elevator that moved four stories down into the ridge that the base was built into. Cassie shivered, partly nervous about being buried in the earth, and partly excited about seeing Mick.

After exiting the elevator, Wallace turned down another hallway and pressed his palm to a panel next to a door. Then a scanner surveyed his right eye stalk. Then a small speaker sounded with a tinny voice.

"Who is it?"

Snailman sighed. "You know the official protocol, Agent Johnson."

"Who is it, *Agent* Cooper? I was in the middle of writing a fight scene. You know how hard those are. Why are you here?"

"To see Michael Bruno, alias Swipe, for the purposes of training ... new personnel."

Cassie scoffed quietly. There was no way she would be new personnel with the government. Not after what Anda had told her a few days ago.

"Come in."

The lock clicked.

Snailman muttered, "If only she didn't have a rare power."

He stomped into the room with Cassie trailing behind.

So that's why she's here. Rare powers that could be understood were allowed.

Rare powers like hers were dangerous. Something to be locked away and controlled, no matter if it was the feds or a corporation.

The room before them opened into a round entryway with hallways branching off in all directions. At the center was a huge desk with six large flat-screen monitors, and several smaller ones scattered around. An agent sat before them, studying the monitors. As Cassie walked closer, she could see multiple navigation mice flickering between them. Only one seemed to coordinate to the woman's hand on the mouse. The other cursors seemed to move on their own—or maybe in connection with her gaze?

She spun around in her gamer chair to face Cassie.

"You're shorter than you look on screen." The heavyset, brown-skinned woman stared at her over rectangular black glasses.

Unlike the standard uniform of gray and blue clothes or business attire, she was clad in leggings, a long black tunic with gold Star Trek insignias all over it, and a yellow cardigan. "They're playing ads for you all over the radio stations, streaming services. They even have ads on social media and search engines."

Augh, why? Contrary to popular opinion, there was something known as bad publicity. Power-Up Publicity was excelling at it right now. Every moment they painted her as the damsel in distress in the hands of a supervillain made things even worse for her going public. They had a stranglehold over the narrative.

Tendrils of electric energy tickled her senses from the bank of flat-screen monitors and hard drives behind Agent Johson. Cassie clenched her hands together, resisting the urge to fiddle with the ribbons and strands. This was not the time to lose control.

She finally responded, pitching her voice light. "I guess Power-Up Publicity has the budget to waste."

"Hmph." She flipped a black twisted lock of hair behind her shoulder, then turned in her chair to face Snailman. "You sure about this, Wallace? I don't want any trouble from the higher ups. Not after Robin sneaked out and knocked a glass of water onto someone's workstation in accounting."

As if hearing its name, a tail flicked out from below the desk. Cassie peeked down to see a cat with patches of calico and tabby patterns on white fur curled up on a hard drive. The kitty clearly needed to be petted right now.

Snailman nudged her. She straightened up again, pulling her arm away just before stroking Robin's back.

"It will only be for thirty minutes. Additional training might be useful should the General Chamber approve Special Agent Garvey's request to add Mr. Bruno to a team."

"Oh, they'll approve it." She snorted. "They let me on, after all. Along with Robin and Blade."

"Blade?"

"He's over in the corner. Mick already wore him out playing with him this morning." She coughed. "I mean, exercising Mick's genner abilities."

Cassie glanced over to see a long-haired mini dachshund curled up on a gray dog bed next to the desk, his narrow head propped up on a pillow shaped like Pikachu.

Her heart melted even further, both at the cute animal and the thought that Mick had been playing with him. "He's adorable!"

"Isn't he? Can't be left alone either. Both of them kept me company around the house before Gendep made me a salary offer I couldn't refuse. I have two kids in college and one running a start-up in board games."

"Oh, what kind? Tabletop RPG? Deck builder? Party?"

Her face lit up. "Mostly Devon is developing word and puzzle games, although I think he's working on a cooperative game. As a matter of fact—"

Wallace cleared his throat. "Another time, Paula. Please teleport us into his cell."

"Oh, I don't need to." She turned back to the computer bank. "He's been cleared for a regular cell. With that neuralepser on, he isn't considered a major threat anymore." She pointed down the gray cinderblock hallway to the door nearest to the entryway that held her massive desk. "I'll buzz you in."

As the agent turned back to her monitors, Cassie inhaled, then exhaled slowly. Finally, she would get to see him. They paused before the steel door.

A buzzer sounded. "Mick! You have company."

The door slid aside, revealing a large, empty room in front of the doorway.

At least they gave him some space. It was larger than the military-issue room that she ignored in favor of Katrina. If she was going to be cramped, she'd rather it be in her own campervan.

She ran into the room. "Okay, where are you?"

"The room isn't that big, Cass." The warm, dry voice sent a thrill through her veins. Mick rose from a bed pushed against the wall wearing the same standard-issue, boring clothes. "Although maybe it is for shorties like you."

His brown eyes glinted as he took her in, a small smile curving his lips.

Cassie grinned. "We'll see about that."

She ran across the room and jumped at him. Hopefully he would catch her. After all, he prided himself on quick reflexes.

As his arms encircled her, holding her close as her legs wrapped around his waist, she whispered in his ear, "Ready to break out of here?"

Chapter Twenty-Two

Her words echoed through him, bringing relief as well as happiness.

Mick wasn't stupid. She was whispering for a reason, which meant that she had news. Potentially awful news.

But he wouldn't complain that communicating this information involved close proximity. He wasn't much for that in general. But Cass was different.

"It's about time," he answered with equal softness, studying her heart-shaped face again. "What did you learn?"

"Anda can't help me. I'm too weird, and my powers can't be read by any devices or easily analyzed, which means I'm not a great recruit for Team Government Genners. If some of the General Chamber found out, it would make them nervous. They'd probably lock me away in a cell for additional study."

"The hell they will." It was bad enough that he was shut up in here. Mick gave a short laugh. "Didn't know you *wanted* to join up with a government team."

"Obviously, I did." She rolled her eyes. "Anda's become more of a control-freak over the years. Super stressed-out too. We weren't in her plans, and then she tried to shove us into her plans and that isn't going so well."

"Well, she wasn't in our plans either." The woman was a menace.

"We had plans?"

"Enough of them."

Her eyes twinkled. "Yeah, I mentioned the whole abducted-by-the-feds issue." She tapped on his shoulders. "I'm learning how to use my abilities."

He nodded. "Enough to be useful?"

"Soon."

It was refreshing to talk to someone who understood the shorthand for criminals and villains. Someone who knew that 'being useful' meant using abilities to get out of there. Someone who had zero problems with running from a government facility and the dubious protection it provided.

"What about you?" She tapped his chest, the spot heating under her touch. Exactly where the spine tattoo was. "They might offer you a deal to clear your record."

"I can live without it. I don't go for traditional jobs anyway." He winked.

Cass raised her eyebrows. "But still heroic ones, right? After all, I am your superhero publicist."

"Says the woman trying to escape the heroes."

"It's called freelancing, you dingbat." At her pert, inviting look, he leaned in closer. Her lips parted.

A nasal voice interjected, "This is not additional training."

Screw it. He captured her mouth in a brief kiss that she returned firmly.

"Finally," she breathed as they pulled apart. Then she gave him a peck on the nose. "Until next time."

Man, it was unfair how she could make him feel like this. Completely out of his head, away from rational thoughts. Only focused on her.

Actually, he felt better. Freer than he had in days.

"Do I need to start sliming you?"

Mick reluctantly set Cassie on the ground, then leveled a stare at Snailman. "Take off my neuralepser, and I can outrun whatever you throw at me."

The stupid piece of metal was the bane of his existence. Along with this whole cell. The only thing that had kept him going the last five days was pondering ways to escape, what to do next, and where he stood with Cassie.

And the dog. Blade the dachshund made everything better.

He reached back to touch the small, penny-sized implant. Something felt ... different.

Snailman's eye stalks swiveled dismissively. "Not in here. The space is too limited. You would fail easily and quickly."

"We could try and see."

"Whoa, you two. It's *my* training session with Mick." Cassie tilted her head, eyeing them. "Although, it would be a fun way to test absorbing kinetic energy." She shrugged. "On second thought, go ahead. Try to hit him with slime."

Mick grumbled. "Just me?"

"You are the two in conflict. I am just an innocent bystander. Besides, Anda's already been throwing rocks at me, along with light beams, cell phones, taser blasts—"

"Hitting you once with a taser wasn't enough?"

"Aha, now I can absorb it." She pursed her lips. "I think she might have regretted that lesson afterward."

He grinned. "That's what you do."

"Right, so I'm just curious if I could absorb the energy and stop the slime before it hits you."

She'd improved that much? Hmmm. He touched the neuralepser again. Maybe Cass was even better than she realized.

Mick eyed her. "Does your training include absorbing energy from objects?"

"Sometimes. Why?" She studied him, gaze unfocused for a moment. "Crap."

"What?" Snailman's voice turned suspicious.

She knew. He could tell from how her eyes narrowed, how she gave a tiny giggle. The minx had disabled his neuralepser. Unintentionally, if the sheepish look on her face was anything to go by.

Which meant he could have fun with the sanctimonious Snailman.

"Nothing," he said quickly. "Go ahead. Fling the slime. If you can catch me."

"There's no reason I can't catch you."

"Then try it."

"Fine. It's your loss when you have to use the solvent to clean it off."

He reached out, hands splayed, and aimed a stream of slime at

Mick's chest. He felt himself effortlessly enter that space between seconds where he could move fast. Faster than the plodding, slithery slime. Faster than the superhero who wielded it.

Effortlessly, he moved out of the stream. The next second, it fell to the ground in a sticky mess, thanks to Cass's powers.

"What was that?" Snailman glared at him, then Cass. "The neuralepser—you did this! You talked me into letting you down here so you could disable it."

"No, it was an accident. They should put warning labels on kisses." Cassie blinked. "Anda did say that my powers might unlock more around people that I'm comfortable with."

"But this—"

The intercom crackled.

"Calm down, Agent Cooper," Paula intoned. "You're still locked in the cell. And it doesn't look like Cassie or Mick are going to try anything. Are they?"

Mick paused. "I mean—"

"No." Cass moved toward him and shoved him. "That's not what we do."

"What happened to breaking out?"

"It was a metaphor. Definitely a metaphor."

She shook her head slightly and mouthed something that seemed like *not now*. He sighed. Of course. Cass hadn't actually planned it yet. It seemed like she hadn't had much time to plan anything. They'd always come up with the best schemes together. Being shut up on the base wasn't helping either of them.

They needed out. He'd already been considering which safe

house would be best.

"Whoa," Paula's voice sounded over the intercom. "New update on Power-Up Publicity. Gavyn Fields cancelled several appearances due to poor health. Rumors are that the strain of searching for Ms. Robinson has been too much—oh, the news is playing it like you and him were secret lovers. Nothing official on that. His dad Max is offering three million now for your return. He says there's a lead on the villain responsible for it, and he's going live at a press conference in seven days."

Mick ground his teeth. His biological father knew exactly what he was doing. He jacked up Donny on more serums betting that Mick would be compelled to help him.

"Unbelievable!" Cass threw up her hands. "The government just sits on their hands and ignores the press—while that corporate creep shoves me into a relationship rumor and seems ready to screw over Mick! Plus, who knows what's going on with Donny. No. This is not going to happen."

"It already has," Snailman said.

"It won't go any further." She turned on him. "Get us a meeting with Anda. Now."

He spluttered. "Your sister is very busy—"

"Then I'll be very busy absorbing as much energy as I can, and then Mick and I will handle this on our own."

Mick grunted in agreement. "The meeting is just a courtesy. I'd take it because I'm going to help my brother, regardless."

"You dare threaten me?"

"Already contacted Special Agent Garvey," Paula said at the

same time. "Sorry, Wallace. I'm with her. The court of public opinion has power. And the government moves slower than a sloth at naptime."

He smiled faintly. *I knew I liked her.*

Snailman exhaled through his teeth. "Fine. Follow me." He jabbed a finger at Mick. "You will not go anywhere else but the conference room."

"Sure." So far. If things went south, he and Cassie were out of here, one way or another.

A short while later, they all gathered in the small conference room. He and Cass sat on one side of the table, and Snailman and Anda on the other.

"I told you, Cassie. There are no other options," Anda insisted. "You have to stay here."

"No, I won't. You might have all the degrees, but I have some too. I know marketing and public perception." She tucked her purple hair behind her ears. "You need evidence. And you need someone inside Power-Up Publicity to get it."

Shock crashed through Mick. She couldn't be serious. He'd spent the better part of eight years staying away from that crap hole.

Anda, likewise, looked ready to argue. Before either of them could speak, Cass barreled on, pushing back her chair and standing up. "The best option here is for me to play into the situation and return. It will give me leverage, especially in the eyes of the media. We'll arrange it to be a public scenario where I'll be found by the press before Power-Up Publicity can whisk me away. I'll use the connection the media are already spinning between Donny and I if I have to."

"Use it how?" Snailman asked. "Do you mean a romantic relationship?" His eye stalks twisted to look at Mick.

"I've seen her flirt her way into a completed research paper," he snorted.

"You have no proof." She rolled her eyes and shoved Mick. "And no. I can play it up as siblings. It's not that hard, especially since Mick and Donny are already siblings."

Was she already hinting at in-law connections?

Then again, he'd let himself get and stay captured for her. Maybe they were on the same page about their future together.

"It won't take that much," Cass continued. "When I get inside, I can get whatever information we need."

Silence fell for a moment. Mick's mind spun as he tried to poke holes in the plan from every angle. This wasn't how things were supposed to go. Cass was free from Power-Up Publicity. She couldn't go back there.

Yet, the plan had some merit. "Max is arrogant and idealistic. I don't think he'll look too closely at the 'why,' at least not at first. It could work."

"I don't like it," Anda muttered, getting to her feet. "You're untrained, Cassie. You're not an agent, you're a civilian."

"You've been training me." She waggled her fingers, flashing a smile.

"Not nearly enough!"

"Since my abilities can't be detected, I can get into Power-Up Publicity without them suspecting anything, which means I have the element of surprise."

"What if you end up stuck there again?" Mick asked, tilting his head back to look up at her. "You're a survivor, Cass. You've proven that, and I saw it when I met you. But that doesn't mean you need to put yourself in danger without backup."

She turned that bright, winsome smile on him, and despite himself, he almost smiled back. Warmth must have showed in his eyes because her smile widened. "Then you'll just have to get me out. Or go in with me, maybe? After all, I need a valiant rescuer, right? It could be part of your journey to hero."

Cass winked at him. The annoying woman. Never mind the heat that filled him as she squeezed his shoulder. "If things go bad, we can figure it out together, with your brother's help and with that tricksy villain brain of yours. We can even get Donny out."

Go back into the lion's den. Face the ass who had kept him imprisoned for two years. Was it the best idea? Maybe not. But it was action. From the look on Cass's face, he knew it would be impossible to talk her out of it.

And it would be satisfying to bring down Max Fields and finally get Donny out of that deathtrap.

"Fine." He stood at last. "I'm in."

Chapter Twenty-Three

"There is no 'in,'" Anda snapped. "You two are here by my good graces—"

"We're here because the government grabbed us," Mick said, crossing his arms. "A branch of the government that still hasn't given us any answers about our status. Now we're offering to help you out, even after we were held without due process by Gendep."

"It's a work in progress!"

Mick scoffed. "Tell that to a lawyer."

Cassie could have kissed him for that. It expressed all the annoyance she'd felt over the last few days but had to suck up because, after all, this was her sister's base. Her highly qualified, highly educated sister with all the degrees and powers. But the situation with Power-Up Publicity had changed from a game of politics to a game of marketing, and that was something Cassie knew. She could handle this.

Anda couldn't. She was in over her head.

Her sister fixed her with a fierce stare, as if daring Cassie to step down. She should know better than that. Cassie only lifted her chin and glared back. She and Mick were doing this mission, whether Anda liked it or not.

At last, Anda blinked and shook her head. "Cassie, aren't you scared of going back? They hurt you."

I'm freaking terrified. God help her. Just the thought of going inside made her skin crawl.

She swallowed. "This is about more than just me. There are others still trapped inside working as supervillain publicists. Plus that whole evil plan of Max Fields's that you mentioned a few days ago. And it's about Donny Fields helping me get out when he didn't have to. It doesn't matter that I'm scared. Stopping evil is more important than my fear."

Mick grabbed her hand. She exhaled slowly, drawing strength from his presence and from sheer inner conviction.

"All right." Her sister nodded slowly. "I don't like it, but I understand. It was one reason I joined Gendep. I wanted to be part of a solution and influence that solution."

"Yeah, the same reason I joined Power-Up Publicity." Cassie gave a short laugh. "Once again, I guess you got the A and I got the D minus."

"Don't think like that. You're in a place to help us take them down." Anda's voice softened to the zen yoga-instructor tone as she swiped through her phone. "My superiors are already asking about my plans, and they want to see you both do something to prove yourselves. This is the perfect opportunity."

Mick huffed. "Always glad to prove my loyalty to the government."

A smile twitched her lips at his deadpan words. Snailman bristled from across the table. "We have the opportunity to be part of a new organization to serve our citizens. This is a great honor!"

"Sure it is. I love risking my life for people who locked me up in a cell."

"You are a criminal!"

"Details, details."

Cassie interjected. "I'm not doing this for the government."

Everyone turned to look at her. Good. They could do that, because she had something to say. "I'm doing it because it is the right thing to do. I'll share my findings, but I'm not working for them, and I don't answer to them."

Anda gave her a thoughtful look. "An independent contractor?"

"Consider the government a client of the very recently established Robinson Superhero Marketing Services, LLC."

"Very well." A glint of approval showed in her eyes.

"So, what about this whole neuralepser issue?" Mick asked. "My powers are fully back now, just so you know."

Cassie waved her hand. "My fault."

Her sister groaned. "Really?"

"Yup. I'm not apologizing either."

"You wouldn't." She turned to Mick. "Turn over enough evidence on Max Fields, and I'll work out the rest."

"What does that mean? He's forced to work for the government?"

Her stomach sank. It was bad enough that her sister was looped into this paper-pushing rigamarole. Now Mick would be roped in.

It wouldn't be the worst result in the world. But it wouldn't be great either.

"I can't." He squeezed her hand. "I'm already a partner with Robinson Superhero Marketing Services, LLC."

A smile stretched across her face. "Oh, you are, huh?"

"Sure, why not? After all, we're taking down Max's company." He mock-glared at her. "Although I'm not handling any of the customer service."

"Loser. Fine." Her heart leaped in her chest. Eventually they would have to talk about all these promises and commitments they were making. That could happen later. "I guess we can both do contractor work for the government using our unique skills and connections."

Anda glanced ruefully between the two of them.

"I shouldn't be surprised. I really, really shouldn't be."

"So that's a yes?"

"If I said no, would either of you listen?"

Mick and Cassie exchanged a look. She shrugged. Honesty could sometimes be the best policy, right?

"I did already mention the idea of breaking out to Mick. With our powers, it could happen."

"That's what I thought." Anda tsked. Then her shoulders relaxed, and a small laugh escaped her, almost as if she was relieved.

What had she said earlier? That if she had known about Cassie's situation and powers, she might not have brought her in at all. That the government had no place for her.

At last, Anda spoke. "I expect a very reasonable fee for your services, Ms. Robinson of Robinson Superhero Marketing Services, LLC."

"Perhaps in turn, we'll get expedited paperwork filing on any business registrations or forms?"

"Don't push your luck."

Chapter Twenty-Four

"Hostile invader continues to loiter on the premises." The AI's voice was primly judgmental.

"What have I ever done to you?" Mick threw up his hands from where he sat in the front passenger seat. Usually, he didn't take tech issues personally, but this was ridiculous. He glanced at Cass. "I thought you and Anda programmed her to accept me."

Cass shrugged, her eyes focused on the rain-streaked windshield ahead of her. Katrina wouldn't tolerate Mick going near the steering wheel. "We did our best, but Katrina's been offline for a number of years, and she's apparently developed some quirks."

The AI gave a mechanical chirp. "I have adapted to the inclement circumstances, which is in alignment with my programming. I am not convinced that the individual Michael Bruno, alias Swipe, poses no threat to my mandate of protecting you. He does not even have suitable employment."

"Oh my gosh, are you kidding me?" Cass exclaimed, turning around a tight corner in the old industrial park. It was situated on the outskirts of St. Louis with a forgettable name and a handful of unimpressive signs plastered on various buildings. "Why does his job matter?"

"He is a known thief and criminal associated with numerous gangs."

"He's been *pardoned*." Anda managed to negotiate that in exchange for Mick working with the government as an informant on this mission. The special agent had talked up his significant speedster powers and his willingness to change. The whole idea still made Mick uneasy, but at least it wasn't long-term. He would be working with Cass at her new business once this whole mess was over.

Besides, he was a little tired of always being seen as the bad guy. It made rescues inconvenient. Being an independent contractor was a reasonable substitute. He took a swig of the cold coffee he'd been nursing on the drive.

"His record still makes him an unacceptable companion in this vehicle and an inappropriate potential consort."

Mick spluttered coffee, along with a garbled, "What?"

"Now he defaces the interior of this vehicle. Another mark against him."

"It takes five seconds to clean up," he grumbled, swiping at the console in front of him with a handful of paper napkins. "Who made you a matchmaker?"

"That. What he said." He turned to see Cass swerve around a pothole. "Not that we're ... official, but ... it's my choice. My decision. Not yours."

"I am merely trying to protect you." Did the AI sound a touch petulant?

Cass sighed. "Which is why I never took any dates back to the van."

"An unwise action."

"You're an unwise action." She grinned at Mick. "I seriously didn't remember that she had this protocol. It's been a while since I've ... since, um. Yeah." She looked back at the road. "What are we, anyway? Wait, bad time to ask that question, probably. Focus on getting to the nefarious gangster who is actually a violent criminal."

Mick's lips twitched. "On his bad days."

They hadn't had much time to think about anything over the last week except preparing for this mission. Cass had been focused on training as much as she could, including reviving her childhood marksmanship skills, and he'd been handing over as much intel to the feds as he'd felt comfortable with in exchange for the pardon—as well as proof of the many times he hadn't, in fact, been a supervillain. Especially not lately, and definitely not the kind of villain they were most worried about. Because the neuralepser didn't work, he'd been kept in his cell, and his time with Cass had been limited to training sessions, mealtimes, or planning sessions supervised by Snailman or Anda. Not a single chance to get in another kiss. They'd left this morning with no time for a single stop. The White Coat gang were big on punctuality, especially their accountant.

He studied Cass as she drove down another alley, her olive-toned face made-up and tight with concentration, and her purple hair pulled back in a sleek ponytail again. They'd have find some time to figure out what they were besides friends who were sticking together no matter what. He wouldn't mind adding 'friends that made out' or even 'friends that ended up married and bothering each other for the rest of their lives' to that in the future. But they had to survive the present.

"Stop here. Park near that light pole." Mick pointed to the fixture. "I'll go the rest of the way on foot."

"All right." Cass moved the van into position, then shut off the engine. The light above them flickered in the dismal evening rain. She grimaced and reached her hand toward it. The next second, the light shut off completely. Cass hummed to herself. "Better. I was getting a little drowsy, and the sputtering was bothering me." She turned in her seat to face him, tugging down her black blazer. A hint of uncertainty flitted over her features. "This will work, right?"

Three minutes to the meet. He had time, at least for her. "You're the one who came up with the idea."

"Yeah, I know. I just didn't ... now that we're here ..." She played with the spine pendant around her neck. "Beams don't run into battle. We stay hidden and safe. Maybe ..." She fidgeted with her fingers. "Maybe this is a dumb idea. Another instance of me rushing into things and putting myself where I don't belong."

"That talk doesn't sound like you. It sounds like your parents." Mick gently captured her hand and squeezed it. "It's a good idea. You know I'd tell you if it was stupid."

She was a survivor. She'd proven that, and her powers were built around it.

Cass raised her eyebrows. "You can be just as impulsive."

"Only when it's smart."

"What was that in seventh grade about 'borrowing' those components from the photo lab for—"

"We started a *small* fire on the edge of campus."

"Medium."

"We put it out." He lightly flicked the tip of her nose. Dang, she was cute. "This is the plan. We go ahead, and if things go to crap, we do something new."

Cass chuckled, the tension easing from her shoulders a little. "Great pep talk."

"I should go into motivational speaking."

"They also need publicists." Before he could react, she leaned forward and gave him a quick kiss edged with longing. He returned it fiercely, for a few seconds wishing they were anywhere but here.

But this was their plan. It needed to go off without a hitch. And there was only a minute and a half left.

"More soon." He tilted his head. "Why isn't your lipstick smeared?"

"Waterproof makeup. I am going to be outside in the rain, after all."

"What's it made of, rubber?"

"Sure, genius. Give the boy a cookie." She rolled her eyes. "Okay, you antagonize the villains, I drop the shiny object in the middle of the big, obvious field that has plenty of space for a hero versus villain battle—"

"Then you get somewhere safe until the fight starts and the camera starts rolling. I'll find you."

"Tada! Heroic rescue of the missing publicist on camera by the guy Max Fields was going to throw on the chopping block." She tapped her fingers on the steering wheel. "It absolutely should work."

"Barely an inconvenience."

With those words and a quick prayer, he left the van.

Ten seconds. Plenty of time.

He spared one of them to make sure Cass was driving toward the field. Then Mick sped off to the meet.

The accountant stood beneath the overhang of a small building advertising shower parts. As usual, he wore rumpled jeans, an old white bowling jacket, and a crisp white shirt underneath. He looked at the face of a shiny Rolex on his wrist.

Mick stopped next to him with one second to spare. "Is that a new one?"

"You know very well I get a replacement every week to ensure the time keeping is optimized." The accountant looked up, his ash-blond hair gelled three inches above his head. He had the kind of jaw and forehead that belonged to a male model, but the squint in his close-set watery green eyes and the off-kilter nose many times broken ruined it. "What is this about?"

"Calling in that favor."

"Favor?"

"The one where I didn't rat you out for embezzling funds from the White Coat accounts to cover your dad's cancer surgery. Or what about when I rescued your cousin out of that ring?"

The accountant scowled. "I thought you turned over a new leaf and found God and the angels and whatever else happens in those cults."

"So now here's a chance to be on the side of the angels." Mick bared his teeth in what was almost a grin. Truthfully, he didn't want to pull a shakedown here. He was past that, and no one he loved was in imminent danger. But the accountant didn't know that, and the White Coat gang was brutal. They could use some justice at the hands of the feds. "Might even get you a way out."

"I don't have enough put away for my weekly fix. But I want left out of the fight."

"No guarantees, but I can give you some tips if you say yes in the next minute."

The accountant squinted at him, then his shoulders slumped. "So, what's the angle? The boss and his circle are due back in ten."

"Nothing major." Mick leaned against the wall, arms folded, the very picture of calm, even while everything in him was twanging with tension. "Just need to get them to take a detour. Trust me, it'll be worth their while."

Chapter Twenty-Five

Cassie pulled over at the edge of the field, a few feet from the dirt-and-gravel road. If the dilapidated business area was on the edge of St. Louis, this nondescript area was on the edge of that area. Part of her knew that choosing a location downtown would get more immediate attention, which was the main goal of this plan. But she couldn't stomach endangering civilians.

Like me. I'm a civilian. Except that she wasn't anymore. She wasn't a bystander helping villains spin their latest exploit for the press or choose a new handle or describe an evil plot in a more appealing manner for potential sidekicks.

She was a genner. A superhero. Sort of.

"A hero pretending to be a civilian to trick and sneak into an evil corporation in order to get dirt and bring them down." Cassie shut off the campervan. "Katrina, how would you describe that?"

The AI was silent for a moment. "That scenario is outside the parameters of my programming."

"That's fair." Cassie sighed. "Okay, time to drop the bait."

She reached under the seat, pulled out a dented black metal container about the size of a shoebox, and checked inside. There was the fuel cell, ready for action. An experimental government device created to explode without leaving any traces behind. No chemicals, no burning smell, nothing. Only a clear plastic cylinder that looked like it belonged to a vacuum tube system for depositing money at a bank. Considering this would be used in urban areas, no one would glance at it twice afterward.

"Government R&D can be scary sometimes," she muttered, closing the box and taking the handle. "Okay, let's do this. Katrina, stealth mode. I'll be back soon."

"Affirmative."

She exited the van, her chunky heels squishing into the soft grass, and the drizzle saturating her clothes. All the better to sell the act of the beleaguered office worker. She exhaled a slow breath and pulled some tendrils of hair free from her ponytail. Thank God she was still warm from the energy she had taken from the streetlight. She would have been shivering uncontrollably otherwise. Now she only trembled a little, which was okay. A bit of shivering would help sell the role.

This had to work. Everything was on schedule. Katrina was out of the way, Mick was bringing in the supervillains, and she was wandering near the staging area, and—

"Oh crap. Checking in." She tapped a tiny flesh-toned device nestled in her ear. "Getting the bait in place, Mindwave, and looking like a rain-drenched rat."

Calling her sister by a codename was weird, especially because the name itself implied she had telepathic powers, not a unique kind of bioelectric energy ability. But Anda had said it was better to be inexact and catch people off guard, and Cassie couldn't argue with that.

"Good job, Enigma." Her sister's voice was zen-like. Speaking of odd code names, since it was better that no one figured out Cassie's abilities, and since she herself was still trying master them, Enigma seemed to be the best fit.

Anda continued. "We're bringing in more contract heroes. ETA of villains?"

"Nine minutes. Probably."

"Probably?"

She shrugged, continuing her trudge across the field. "You knew Mick couldn't wear an earcom in case the gang scanned him. It's my best guess."

"Acknowledged." That was Snailman. "Cameras have been secured in the designated locations. Streaming will commence as soon as the battle starts. Ensure that your struggle is seen by them."

Cassie nodded. "Don't worry, I'll bring the drama as soon as the battle begins."

"Good. Keep lines open until the mark shows up. Over and out."

She dropped the box in a good spot in the field—far enough away from the campervan to avoid being seen, but close enough that she could absorb the energy contained within at just the right time. The villains would blame the device for having a shut-off feature. They wouldn't realize that Cassie was that feature.

And it would notify Power-Up Publicity to notify the contract heroes. Which would guarantee that Max Fields noticed her.

Cassie started walking back toward the campervan. A soft,

tuneless humming slipped out, an attempt to distract herself from the wet and the cold that had begun to work its way through her clothes, despite absorbing the bit of light energy.

Let this work. This had to work.

She paused a few feet from where she could sense the campervan was, although all she could see was a cluster of trees. Her energy sense could detect the truth beneath the holograph. Mom and Dad had really held out on her with the mods on her ride.

The glare of car lights interrupted her thoughts. Pulse jumping, Cassie turned toward the light and took in a cavalcade of SUVs.

Not good. They definitely weren't trying to be subtle. Then again, Mick hadn't chosen the White Coats for subtlety. The whole point of this was spectacle.

"ETA on the heroes?" She asked.

Snailman answered. "Three minutes."

"Looks like the villains are here early."

The doors of the frontmost SUV opened. Two muscled men wearing all white with black leather dusters over top got out, looking around suspiciously.

Right. Because the White Coat gang wore black dusters, except for the leader. Who wouldn't show up for a tip like this. They would send underlings.

Anda's swearing sounded on the earcom. "I'll see if I can rush them. Enigma, keep an eye out. Neutralize the weapon at all costs. Even if the heroes don't show up in time."

"Got it Mindwave."

A total of five thugs exited the SUVs and began stomping across the field, even as the drizzle turned to rain. Some of them definitely had powers—at least one was an energy genner of some kind. Another had the twitchiness of a primal. Gangs often liked to make primals because the animal-based serums were cheaper and the results tended toward instability and violence, making them ideal hitters. She shuddered.

Take your time. Look around. Just wait for the heroes to arrive.

They surrounded the box. One of them brought out a tool for some specialized poking and prodding. Another pulled out a thick, fancy pair of binocular-looking things. Maybe with x-ray vision?

A bit more conversation. Good.

"One minute out."

Cassie squinted at the gangsters. "They're discussing the box. Okay, now one of them is picking it up. Looking it over."

"Thirty seconds."

"They're starting to walk back to the SUVs."

Anda swore again. "We can't take any chances. Neutralize the weapon."

"Will do."

She reached out toward the box, seeking the ribbons of energy that she could see in her mind's eye.

Only, they weren't there. There was nothing.

"Mindwave, the box doesn't have any special features that suddenly activated, does it?"

"Negative."

"Augh. I must be just out of range." She hadn't factored them walking to their car on the other side of the field. "I'm going in closer."

"Be careful, Enigma."

Cassie set her face. "It's an open field and a dangerous weapon. You can get neutralization or caution, but not both."

Between the two, she was going for neutralization. She was one person. That device could take out hundreds, even thousands of people. There really wasn't any argument about which choice to make.

She started across the field, clenching her teeth against the cold rain, her hand now by her side. While having it stretched out was comforting, Cassie didn't need to do it.

As she walked, the energy ribbons started filtering through her awareness. *There you are.*

The energy flowed from the device toward her, moving in powerful waves. She winced, pulling up a technique she'd learned in training to stem the tide. She could only take so much at once. Otherwise, the energy would probably kill her.

The gangsters reached the SUVs. Then one of them looked around—and his eyes focused on her. Which wasn't hard because she was the only figure in the field.

Pistols emerged from black dusters, the barrels aimed at her. Adrenaline kicked through her body. She started backing up. The energy surged into her faster and faster, obliterating all sensation of her chronic pain in heady blasts that overwhelmed her senses.

Her foot fell backward into something, and her ankle twisted painfully. She gasped.

A hole.

Stupid gophers. Or groundhogs or whatever had dug the tiny chasm.

Something flashed above her. A laser blast from some kind of flying genner, complete with a cape.

"Step away from that citizen!"

The sudden shout startled her right onto her butt in the soaking wet grass.

One of the thugs threw off his duster, revealing dragon-like wings. He took off after the flying genner with a roar. More genners swarmed the field, both hero and villain, so fast she couldn't tell the difference. Cassie scooted backward, still filled with the scalding energy from the weapon.

Release it. Have to release it. But where?

Instincts made the decision for her. It flew out of her palms into the ground, bucking the earth a few times. Her shoulders slumped with the sudden loss, but she kept scooting backward. Hopefully no one would tie the ground thing to her. It wasn't that obvious.

Cars skidded to a stop. People with cameras and phones jumped out, already filming the epic battle for their social media platforms or streaming channels.

Good. That was the idea.

Someone zoomed up to her. Cassie grinned. Mick's energy was bright and blaring and the rest of him was a nice vision too. She pulled out her earcom and threw it into the woods—it would get in the way of the next part of the plan—then grabbed his bicep and leaned against him. "Took you long enough."

"Ambush at the gang. Stupid accountant." He grimaced. "Need

a ride? I'm great at escaping the cops."

"Sure! Wait, the cops?" Cassie turned to face a sea of flashing red-and-blue lights. At least three police cars there to monitor the battle. It was already cooling down. Most of the White Coats had fled the scene, while others were in the final stages of capture.

It was time for the next steps. "We're supposed to be public."

Mick snorted. "Publicly taken in for questioning?"

"Take me in your arms."

"You keep finding excuses for me to do that."

"You have nice arms, and I have a twisted ankle. It's a good fix." She winked. "I'll just claim you're my rescuer and refuse to leave. They can't make me."

"If they try?"

She sighed. "Then we do it your way, villain in shining armor."

Chapter Twenty-Six

She felt good in his arms. Solid and petite and soft in all the right places. It almost made up for how dumb this plan was. Sure, Mick had agreed to it in theory, but now facing all the uniformed officers, every part of him was screaming to run.

"It would be so easy," he muttered. He didn't enjoy standing in the rain either.

Cass shook her head. "We stop running. We infiltrate, we get answers, we find Donny, and we stop the bad guys."

"Unless the cops start firing."

"Unless that."

The officers had their pistols pointed at him. A female officer shouted, "Put the woman down and put your hands up where we can see them."

"No!" Cass yelled back. "I'm too tired to move. And he isn't a villain. He rescued me."

"Ma'am, respectfully, the man holding you is a criminal."

Her hands covered his chest, right where the spine tattoo was. "Check your records. He's been pardoned."

A male officer opened his mouth to argue further. By then, some of the bystanders had moved over to the new event, phones out and recording.

"Wait!" A man pushed his way through the crowd, gripping an umbrella. Mick narrowed his eyes. The silver hair, square face, and authoritative way he moved were all a dead giveaway. Max Fields, in a tailored greatcoat that most likely hid another pinstripe suit.

Mick's stomach clenched. He'd spent years being held by his father, finally managed to escape, and was now walking back into captivity. But he didn't have to like it.

Max gestured at Mick—or maybe at Cass? It was hard to tell. "That's Ms. Cassandra Robinson, my employee who was kidnapped. He found her."

"Are you accusing him, sir?"

Max studied him carefully, then seemed to make a decision. "No. Someone sent me the video of her being kidnapped by a gang, and he wasn't on that video. He did not harm her."

Another officer spoke up, working his way through to the front. "I checked the database. We're still waiting on confirmation, but it appears that Michael Bruno has been pardoned, as the woman claimed."

Cass rubbed her head into his shoulder. "I told you." Then she leaned back and shuddered, her eyes fluttering shut for a moment.

Mick held her closer. "She needs to get inside and get warm."

"I can arrange all that." Max's face softened. "It's the least I can do after what she's been through."

"You could do more," Mick retorted. Then, with more effort, "Let her work as a superhero publicist like she wanted to from the start."

There. He could play along with the plan, even though he just wanted to get out of this whole situation.

I'm doing this for Donny. For the publicists stuck in that basement. For Cass. Because, in the end, he was a good guy. Mostly.

The CEO's expression turned thoughtful. "I could. That might make the rest—" He cut off and nodded. "Bring her to my car. I'll ensure she is cared for."

"Mick ... comes with me ..." How did Cass go from being so loud to sounding so pathetic? The woman should have been an actress. "Please."

A few of the police and all of the bystanders looked at Max. Murmurs of "She's been through so much" and "Isn't it sweet how he's holding her?" filtered through the crowd.

Max sighed and ran his hand through his hair.

"Very well," he said briskly. "Let's go."

Mick wound his way through the cops and cars and shouts of questions from the phone-camera holders. He stopped in front of a fancy black car with a driver and three doors on either side. The driver opened the door, and Mick sat inside on the leather seat, settling Cass beside him. The CEO got in on the other side of the car, facing them.

"Take us to my estate," Max intoned.

"Right away, sir."

Mick's shoulders tightened as the car started up silently and eased out onto the road. It was still a prison, even if it had fancy upholstery and a minifridge.

"Michael," he continued in a polished voice, "it's been a

long time. I didn't expect to find you playing the hero to Ms. Robinson."

"Old friends," he answered shortly. "And I think we can drop the Ms. Robinson."

Max turned to Cass, the slightest quirk to his eyebrows in a question. "Oh? Is there something you wish to reveal?"

She gave a tired smile. "I think you know already, Mr. Fields. I'm Cassandra Liwanag Beam. You can call me Cassie. You went to MIT with my parents, and they disagreed with your methods for working with genners."

"A very polite way of putting it, and certainly not what they said. Please, call me Max." He reached into the minifridge and pulled out a glass bottle of water. "Refreshment for either of you?"

"Thank you."

"I'll pass." Mick glowered. How she could manage the gracious tone was beyond him.

Cass took a careful sip of water. "Very clean, crisp flavor."

"It is one of my favorites." He took a bottle of his own. "So, Ms. Beam, since you seem aware of our connected history, and it seems you endured unfortunate treatment in a certain part of my company, why return?"

"Well, Mick did rescue me. We discovered the truth through some conversations with my sister. Which also" —her lips twisted— "revealed that my family lied to me about their own powers my entire life. No one knows where my parents are. My own abilities are apparently latent but haven't emerged. My sister and I find ourselves on opposite sides of this situation. She seeks out vengeance, whereas I seek out reconciliation." She gave him another smile, slightly strained. "I figured I would return to Power-Up Publicity in hopes of establishing a mutually beneficial situation. All of my work history is with your company."

He tilted his head, a pleased gleam in his gray eyes. Blast it, Cass was right. This was all feeding into his father's ego about how the world should run. The fact that she was demanding a negotiation instead of throwing herself at his mercy seemed to make it even better. "Interesting. You're a wise woman. What are the terms you suggest?"

"As Mick said, I want a position working with superheroes. I want out of the basement and into a well-appointed office. With windows."

"We can arrange that easily, along with an assistant. We can also offer you a furnished apartment and vehicle."

"No, thank you." Her voice turned colder but remained sweet-toned. Cass took another sip of water, holding the pause for a moment. "I will stay in my own accommodations on my own terms, choose my own health care and benefits, and operate with autonomy in my private hours. I will also direct a project to organize better working arrangements for the supervillain publicists."

Max cleared his throat. "You are, of course, welcome to try. We do aim to take the best care of our supervillain publicists. But supervillains are demanding clients with demanding temperaments. And they invest well in the company."

Cass fixed him with a firm stare. "If you allow

supervillains to treat your employees like garbage, how long before they treat your entire business that way? As you said, they have particular—sometimes unstable, psychopathic, homicidal—temperaments. How long before they decide destroying a whole building wing or branch office suits their plans?"

Max's fingers tightened on his bottle. Was she getting to him? Or had some supervillains already done that? Mick suppressed a sigh. It would be just like Max to end up in killer deals. "An interesting point. Anything else?"

"That's all I have for now. You, Mick?"

"Yes, Michael. Do you have any requests?" His lips twitched. "Interesting how your record is now pardoned."

"Expunged as well." Mick managed a smirk. "When I came in for a consult with Cass, I was considering going hero."

"Oh!" He drew out the word, his eyes getting that gleam again. *He really does have a vision of a heroic dynasty.* "Is that still one of your goals?"

"I might have some reasons to switch sides."

Max smiled knowingly. "Yes, it seems you do. Well, as my son, you're welcome to make use of whatever services you find necessary in your new life. I think once the papers are drawn up, an official press conference would be fitting to announce these promising changes. After all, we want to ensure that the public knows which side you both are on." He raised his bottled water. "To this new journey together."

Cassie raised her bottled water as well. "To new journeys." She nudged Mick.

"Hmph. To that."

I'm doing this for Donny. I'm doing this for justice. I'm doing this to get dirt on Max and hand his ass over to the government. He turned to look out the window, both to get his bearings and to avoid punching Max in the nose.

Bringing down his company would have to suffice.

Chapter Twenty-Seven

From a cramped, windowless room with a heavy steel door to a corner office with views of St. Louis, including the Arch a few blocks down. Cassie stared at the monument, sunlight glinting off the edge of the pane. It was unreal, all of this. Especially how fast it had happened.

Three days ago, she had been taken to Max Fields's private estate, ushered to a palatial guest room, and been checked over by the family's private doctor. Including a subtle scan for abilities with a device that the older woman claimed was a new kind of thermometer. Cassie's energy perceptions knew better—and her powers had clamped tightly around her, leading to a negative response on the device. Thank God. The whole point of this plan was infiltration and stealth.

Even more miraculous, Mick had been placed in an adjacent room. Anda had come through in getting his pardon, and the government had changed all the paperwork and digital files in record time. It only meant one thing: the government saw Power-Up Publicity as a real threat. They needed Cassie and Mick to get them more intel and if possible, turn any of her fellow Power-Up Publicity employees.

Her stomach knotted. Cassie inhaled and exhaled, forcing her shoulders to relax. She was due for the official press conference in an hour with Gavyn Fields, Max Fields, and Mick, announcing her rescue and new position at Power-Up Publicity. The media would eat it up and probably play more into her connection with Mick. It would be a PR boost for Power-Up Publicity across the board.

The knots twisted tighter as she strolled over to the large wrap-around desk made of mahogany. It dwarfed her form, even with the equally large, impressive office chair with excellent back support. She had a laptop and two desktop monitors, an assistant she shared only with two other publicists, and a small cooler that was constantly stocked with water in glass bottles, seltzer, fresh fruit, charcuterie, and chocolate truffles.

Cassie smoothed down her dark green blazer and skirt and plucked at the collar of her blouse. She needed to get the fidgets out now. There would be no place for them in front of the press. Nor would it be appropriate to pace the hallways and give her new coworkers more to stare at and whisper about. At least she still had Katrina out there somewhere. Mick said that Anda had found the campervan at the edge of the field, then her sister had parked it in a safe location. Cassie would be able to spend nights there or at Mick's other St. Louis safehouse if necessary. It apparently had multiple rooms and he would ensure one of those rooms had a comfortable mattress and pillows.

More reasons to keep him around.

The alert on her desk buzzed.

"Mr. Bruno to see you, Ms. Robinson."

"Send him in please, Mr. Hendrix."

Cassie grinned despite her nerves, shifting back and forth in her heels, almost in a little dance. Then she stopped, frowning. Her ankle was still a little tender. Ah well, it could deal. Later she could experiment with sending more energy to cool the inflammation.

Mick sauntered in wearing dark jeans, a black t-shirt, and a black leather jacket. It all looked great against his tanned skin. He'd joked about it being his official hero uniform. Cassie couldn't argue with that.

He gave her a once-over in turn, then another. "Heels are dumb, especially with your ankle."

"Your eyes didn't say that." She put her hands on her hips, then perched on the edge of the desk.

"You look gorgeous. They're still dumb."

"Well, it's a free country, and I get to wear dumb heels if I want."

Mick walked closer to her. "Fair. I'm here to escort you to my evil dad so he can show you off in front of the press, so I'm probably just as dumb."

"Probably." She tilted her head, staring up at him. "Although it's also my opportunity to show off one of the newest heroes at Power-Up Publicity, who just so happens to be my client."

"Yeah, client. Among other things." He moved to stand with his hands on either side of her, braced on the desk, his ever-present motion energy flickering off him and constantly teasing at her powers.

"Uh-huh." Her breath shallowed. Mick was referring to their roles as spies, obviously. As members of a secret infiltration team.

Obviously.

She was fine with kissing and flirting, but long-term future planning wasn't a great idea right now. She and Mick had a mission to accomplish, a side hustle to establish with their own business, and a whole family history to unravel. And he still had a lot of baggage. So did she.

Yet, Cassie couldn't help imagining that future anyway.

"We should go," he said, whispering inches away from her lips.

"Mmhmm."

Then his mouth was on hers for an intense kiss that lit her veins on fire, and her fingers found their way through his black hair.

A buzz broke them apart. Cassie put a hand to her pounding heart.

"Yes?"

"Mr. Gavyn Fields awaits you in the lobby."

"Thank you, Mr. Hendrix."

All interest faded from Mick's expression, replaced by a tight look of concern. She knew it well.

Donny was awake. They would finally see him and assess how bad his physical health was, to say nothing of his mental health. Plus, Donny didn't know about the plan. Somehow, they needed to tell him.

Mick backed away. She slipped off the desk, tugging at her blazer. Her hand fluttered over her face.

"Don't worry, your rubber makeup is fine." He winked.

"Shut up." She swatted him. "I'm just glad we dealt with the bugs and trackers in this room."

"What are friends for, if not for getting rid of illegal surveillance tech?"

As they left the office, Cassie felt her usual mask of perky professionalism fall into place, and Mick followed her with his slight rebel swagger. Everything was normal. Just a publicist and her superhero client.

For now, anyway.

She sighed as she walked across the main lobby of Power-Up Publicity and slowed to greet Angus, whom she had yet to see since her return to the corporation.

Angus, who looked an awful lot like an older version of Herbert, the man in the picture with her parents and Mitty Feldmann, aka Max Fields.

"How are you doing today, Angus?"

"Oh, I'm doing fine, Ms. Robinson." His raspy voice was as welcoming as ever. He returned her smile. "How's your family?"

Had he asked that on purpose? Cassie's usual reply caught in her throat. "Pretty well."

"Make sure to give them my regards." The bald man studied her intently for a moment, his bronze eyes thoughtful. "You may not realize this, but we go way back."

"Oh, really?" She raised her eyebrows, playing along.

"Yes. Although I differed with your folks over a few things, including how to handle opposition." He shrugged.

"Opposition?" Cassie stared. Was he really going to give her the information here? No way. Life didn't work that easily.

"You don't want to be late, miss." He nodded to where Gavyn

Fields stood at the door. Then Angus eyed Mick. "You keep taking care of her, all right?"

"Yes, sir." Mick's voice was earnest and firm.

"Good. I'll see you both soon."

"Right. Soon."

Cassie pivoted back to the lobby, her mind spinning.

The mission had gotten even more interesting.

I don't believe in cliffhangers. Nope. Absolutely not.

But I did almost get there with this one, mwahaha. Yes, I am actively working on the next books.

In the meantime, I'd love your feedback in a review! Giving reviews is a wonderful superpower readers have. Feel free!

Also, if you want exclusive behind-the-scenes info on the world of The Superhero Publicist—including character aesthetics, playlist, and deleted scenes—scan the QR code below to sign up for my newsletter (you also get updates about my books, plus special deals).

Or if you feel like typing:
https://skilled-artisan-2780.ck.page/superpublicist

If you're a fan of the level of snark in this book and also love urban fantasy, check out The Steel City Genie, my urban fantasy series.

Need more superheroes? My friend H.L. Burke has so many epic superhero books. Really. There's like over 18 of them now. Plenty to binge read. Just go to H. L. Burke on Amazon.

Go forth and be awesome!

Acknowledgements

Eternal gratitude to God, who continues to inspire every story I write.

A massive shout-out to my husband Stephen, who helped me figure out some tangled issues with this story (and had fun doing it).

Super thanks to author and dear friend H.L. Burke, who was super-encouraging as I joined the ranks of superhero authors (which is super-awesome).

All the gratitude to alpha readers Sarah Delena White, Hannah Wilson, Jessica Fry, and Stars for reading all the inbox excerpts and enjoying them (even when I accidentally send you the same ones a few times).

Much gratefulness to superb beta readers Madeline Martin, Allison Ohl, Rachael Barcellano, Veronica Lynn, Cathrine Bonham, and Heidi Lyn Burke. Your feedback was so helpful and amazing.

Much thanks to editor Sarah McConahy for diving into this new genre with me! You make all my stories better.

A huge pile of confetti to Kristen Hildebrand for the amazing illustration—you are a true gift to work with. And so much appreciation for Sabrina Watts of Enchanted Ink Studio, who zeroed in on the right typography when I was going "um, it's like this, but not really."

Finally, all the thanks to my faithful readers. I'm truly blessed to know you and every day I'm so psyched that you love my words. Enjoy! (And yes, more books are coming).

About the Author

Janeen Ippolito writes marvelous misfits and heroic tricksters. She's an award-winning author of over 20 books, including urban fantasy, steampunk fantasy, fairy tales, and superheroes. She's also an experienced editor, coach, and marketing strategist at Author Elevate, where she equips fiction authors for sustainable success. You can find her hanging out at the Author Elevate YouTube Channel featuring author interviews, savvy author tips, and 3 Random Question book features. In her spare time, she sword fights, plays ukulele, and reads whatever she feels like. She loves to collaborate and encourage, so connect with her on social media or at jiauthor.com.